Nefarious Endeavors

Jeremy Void

Other books by Jeremy Void

Derelict America
short stories and essays

Smash a Lightbulb
Poetry for Lowlifes
poetry, prose, creative essays, and more

Erase Your Face
The SkullFuck Collection
visual poems

Just a Kid
experimental prose and poetry

www.chaoswriting.net

Nefarious Endeavors

2nd edition

Jeremy Void

Nefarious Endeavors

ChaosWriting Press first edition / 20014

ISBN Number:
978-0-578-16465-6

ChaosWriting **Press**

IT'S A MINDFUCK

www.chaoswriting.net

To my parents

Jeremy Void is NOT liable for any misdeeds performed after reading this book. If you even think about suing him for your own stupidity, someone may or may not break into your home at night and put a bullet in the back of your head while you sleep.

Contents

I pledge defiance to the government of the United States of America and the injustice for which it stands; one nation above God, divisible and quite corruptible, with liberty and justice for some.

sanity comes in small doses

Acknowledgements

A **special thanks to all** those who made this book possible—to God for blessing me with this brilliant ability to manipulate words; to Tomás, and Robert, and Steve for giving me honest feedback, both good and bad, about my stories; to my parents for generously covering the publishing costs; to Sharon for facilitating a group for writers and allowing me to attend and for the general feedback given to me to better my stories; to the rest of my Creative Writing group; to Dominique for helping me to find my voice; to Charity for challenging me in ways I haven't been challenged much before; to the Rutland Punk scene— "This one goes out to the Punks: we RULE the fucking world"; to anybody else who supported me along the way; and, last but not least, to all those who doubted me and thought of me as only a fuckup who would amount to nothing. Again, thanks for everything. And just because (if) I did not mention you specifically does not in any way, shape, or form mean you were not important in the making of this book, because I could not have done this alone.

Jeremy Void

Preface

I've been thinking really hard about what to write here, possibly over-thinking it. I seem to have writer's block but still want to go forth in publishing this book. I get writer's block on occasion. Some say writer's block doesn't exist, but for me it does. Maybe one day I'll be able to master these bouts, but for now it's a reality and there's not much that can be done about it.

Since I have to write something here—or at least since I want to and feel it would be beneficial to—I've decided to treat this section as a journal entry, a stream-of-conscious entry, and pretty much just write what comes to mind, as I'm doing now.

This collection is darker, fiercer, crazier, and much more intense than my last collection. These stories, I'd like to think, ask questions, break rules, and are not meant to be taken seriously. I'm not a racist, I'm not a bigot; in fact, my mind is extremely open and willing to hear adverse points of view, opinions I might not agree with.

My past life consisted of nothing good, nothing worth admiration, but if it weren't for that, I wouldn't have brought you this— this book, *Nefarious Endeavors*. Someone once asked me what the craziest thing I've ever done was, and after thinking long and hard about what it could be, I offered up an answer. He told me I was wrong, and I cursed him out for challenging me. Not really, though, but instead I challenged him, asking *him* what the craziest thing I've ever done was, then, if he was so damned smart.

He told me it was that I drank, that I did drugs, because if it weren't for those two components, none of my crazy behavior would have existed.

Or would it?

When I was nineteen, I went and took a neuro-psych test. If you don't know what that means, it's basically when someone, usually someone sick in the head, meets with a psychologist they've never met before. The psychologist administers a series of tests that take place over the course of two days. Have you ever heard of "Ink Blots"? Well, that's one of the tests.

The reason I agreed to doing this was because my girlfriend's mom had a DSM book (Diagnosis and Statistics Manual of Mental Disorders). Curious about what was truly wrong with me, she opened the book to the page about antisocial personality disorder. It stated that to be properly diagnosed with said disorder I must fit six or seven out of the ten symptoms. She read each symptom to me and I think I was one short of meeting the criteria. The reason why I fell short like I did was because the other symptoms didn't apply to me. For example, I was never married, and one symptom was that I had been divorced.

Preface

Next she flipped the pages to borderline personality disorder, a step down from antisocial, and I had one symptom over the minimum. Again, the symptoms that didn't fit me didn't apply to me.

So I went in and got my head checked.

I spent two days with that doctor.

He diagnosed me with: borderline personality disorder with antisocial and psychotic features.

Just like I had expected.

One of the tests he administered was to show me a still photograph and I had to tell him what happened before the picture was taken and after it was taken. Of course, all of my answers, he commented in the report, consisted of antisocial behaviors.

No surprise there.

One of the pictures was a guy standing up at a window and peering out, and behind him, lying in bed, was a naked woman with one of her breasts exposed. I said he cheated on his wife with a hooker and now stared out the window. Or something like that.

There was one where a guy was loading boxes into a narrow boat, and I said that he was loading either drugs or guns into that boat because he worked for the mob.

Look at me now, you asshole doctor, whose mind is closed; look at the stories I wrote and tell me I'm crazy.

I am crazy, though.

When I was younger I always wanted to write a screenplay. I even started a screenplay about a kid getting sent to rehab. I never finished it, though. I think I gave up when one of my classmates found it on my desk and showed the whole class and laughed at how stupid it was and how stupid I was and blah blah blah.

Jeremy Void

When I was nineteen I wrote the first chapter of what I hoped to be my first novel—the story of my life, a one-chapter wonder. The book would have been called *Testimonies of a Fuckup*. It was based on me, of course, on my life, on my habits, on my behaviors. I don't think I had the capacity then to write about someone else. And up to that point I'd never even read a book, so how was I supposed to write one, then?

It was supposed to be a comedy.

What I find funny, most people find wretched. Which is funny in itself. Pissing people off is my number-one joy in life.

That said, I hope you enjoy this book.

ENJOY!

An American Beauty

A True Account

Dear you,

Remember me? We met on my twentieth birthday, and I asked you to buy me beer. Since you were twenty-three and I learned later that you had the hots for me, you said you would as long as we drank together underneath the bridge. That was when I should have turned my back and instead walked away with Joe and Fink. I should have, but I didn't. I didn't because I wanted beer and you were the only person standing in my way. An obstacle so easy to bypass.

So I took a chance. Oh yes, was it a chance.

You bought me a forty, and the two of us went off to the bridge. Joe and Fink later gave me scoff for this, and I felt like a fool, though I still confided in them what had happened. Confided? I didn't confide in anyone, didn't confide a thing. Just told the story as true as I suppose I could have, and they laughed at me and called me names.

I guess it is funny, the fact that I sold myself for only one forty ounce when I bet I could have asked for more, but it's over now, and we drank together, and you raped me in the dirt right against the wall of the bridge, moaning in a deep, manly voice that scared me senseless, and the way you rode my groin scared me too, and I'm proud to say my dick didn't budge, but rather, stayed flaccid as it entered your pussy because if it had risen it might have broken with the force of your weight.

Ooh, that would have been so painful, I don't know how I would have coped.

I'd find a way, maybe be sent to the hospital, where they'd snap it back in place, and then I'd have to lay low, or not lay at all, while it healed and until I was in good shape again and then I could bang anyone I wanted and I'd be sure glad the whole ordeal was over and I deserved all the taunts Joe and Fink dished out at me.

But that wasn't the strangest thing. The strangest thing to have happened was after it was all done and while we walked back to the Pit. You said something I couldn't get my mind around, not then or now, for what you said stuck in my head like a stick of dynamite and my head inflated with hot air when the flame finished eating the wick and the stick exploded and flared as my ego grew to an epic size. What you said was, you thanked me for showing you a good time. And like I said, my dick didn't even harden, but remained limp as you thrust your fat hips to and fro, humping me as if you were a horny wolf, and all that arose from my frightened self was a fear of uncertainty and the confusion of how I'd ended up here and a wondering realization that I'd sold myself for only one forty ounce of beer which, I might add, tasted like piss and wasn't worth it at all, but still the deal was made that you would buy it for me if, and only if, I agreed to drink it with you, just the two of us, underneath that grimy bridge.

That was my mistake, and I will never make the same err of judgment, not ever, mainly because I am sober now and thank God those days are over now, and now I can live happily without ever having to sell myself again for something so cheap as a forty ounce.

With love,
Jeremy Void

Jeremy Void

Security Guard Gothic

John Karr was patrolling the roof of the parking garage, with a flashlight in hand, lighting up the dark corners where the moonlight couldn't reach. There were not too many places to hide on the roof, so he hopped inside his Security-Mobile, he liked to call it that, and carted down the ramp to the next floor. He didn't get out of the cart here, but instead crept slowly in a circle, keeping the light trained on the shadows, and then rolled down the ramp directly under the last ramp he had ridden down, emerging on the bottom level of the parking garage. He maneuvered himself until he had covered every square inch of the vicinity.

"All clear," he said into his radio. "Over."

"John." The voice came out wrapped with static. *"My wife's water broke,"* it said. *"Can you take it from here? I have to take her to the hospital. Over."*

That was just like Lenny to leave John all alone. But, anyway, John liked the nights to himself; they gave him time to think.

"John?"

"I'll be all right," he said. "Go tell your wife I said congratulations and give her a big kiss for me. Over."

"*Thank you so much,*" the voice spurted in excitement. "*I really mean that. And, again, congratulations on your ninety days. Over and out.*"

John had worked security at the Natick Mall for one whole year now. In fact, tonight was the one-year anniversary of his first day on the job. He really enjoyed this job. He found it mildly relaxing and easy to do. His partner Lenny was a nice guy, and he and his pregnant wife would frequently throw barbecues at their vacation house on the Cape. His boss Henry, though, he was a lot to handle, always looking for an excuse to hassle John. But John had always been able to cope. He and Lenny often joked about Henry in his absence, bringing light to his bothersome conduct.

Before coming to work at the Natick Mall, he had worked as a Boston cop. If he ever had to choose between the two, he would probably pick policing, although policing was only a thing of the past, and something he would never get back, as a result of a bad car accident.

John walked away from the crash with a busted left leg and minor brain damage, and spent the next year and a half on disability until he couldn't take the boredom any longer. He loved being a cop more than anything, and policing was all he had left.

But, unfortunately, his injuries were a liability.

So, here he was, patrolling the parking garage of the Natick Mall.

John rode up to the top floor on the Security-Mobile and parked beside the bridge, which would carry him to the door, which then transitioned him into the food court. Once in there he continued his journey through the center of the mall. He veered right and ventured down a narrow passage, at the end of which he touched his security ID to a small red light, laser-thin, as if someone were pointing one of those pocket-sized laser beams at the playing card-sized gray platform jutting out of the wall right next to the windowless gray door. When the card-reader buzzed and the red laser turned blue, in that short moment before the light changed back to red, he flung the door open and entered what he referred to as his office on Mondays through Fridays, otherwise known as Home Base. It was a small room, Home Base was. There was a wall lined with TV monitors that showed the mall from various angles, with some shots scanning specific spots, the cameras panning around automatically, and some shots were still, the cameras waiting to be manipulated from inside Home Base. There was a table in front of the monitors topped with many controls which not even John knew what they all did, and he didn't want to find out, nor did he really care, for all that really mattered was the joystick that could control the cameras, and the buttons that switched which camera he had under his control.

He sat down in the swivel chair, propped his black boots on the table, and took a big bite of the Big Mac he had bought on his break at the nearby McDonald's—the McDonald's in the mall was closed.

There, on screen number three, something moved.

His body jolted upright, and he watched the screen, studiously, for suspicious activity. When he saw nothing on the screen he proceeded to prop his boots on the table again, and chowed down on his Big Mac, taking an enormous bite which he washed down with a swig of Red Bull from a can, the perfect beverage to keep him awake and alert. The poisonous combination of fat and caffeine felt good as it splashed down his throat, tainting his tongue with Red Bull's bittersweet aftertaste.

After the car accident John had fallen into a terrible depression, and began binge-drinking almost nightly. He had always been a drinker, though, even before the crash, and on special occasions he would even drink to the point of intoxication. But only on special occasions, mind you. After the crash, though, the liquor had taken hold and he'd started drinking religiously. He would even drink Jäger right here in Home Base when neither Henry nor Lenny was around.

Three months ago Henry had caught John drinking on the job and ordered him to attend Alcoholics Anonymous. After only the first AA meeting he'd exchanged alcohol with caffeine—if it wasn't coffee he was drinking, it was Red Bull—and at the meeting this morning he received his ninety-day chip. He had also received plenty of praise from Lenny when he'd arrived at work today and showboated the chip, as if it were made of gold.

There, on screen number two, something moved.

He quickly righted himself, his boots bombarding the floor, and peered observantly at the monitor, where all there was was a dark, empty Filene's Basement. He watched screen number two for longer than he had watched screen number three, but still, nothing revealed itself. He scratched his head, wondering what he had seen.

It would be rare that something was amiss at the Natick Mall, considering nothing had gone awry in all of John's time working here. So from that he reduced the sighting to only a figment of his imagination.

Security Guard Gothic

He bit into the Big Mac, watching all the monitors more closely now—just in case—when a shadow jumped on screen number one. Okay, maybe something did seem a bit iffy, and he had to find out what. He got up then. Without missing a beat he bolted through the door, and as he hurried down the narrow passage he withdrew his gun and crisscrossed his wrists.

He descended the stalled escalator to the first floor and hurried to camera number one, which hung above Hot Topic. Standing outside the gothic clothing store, he thought that the mall manager really had to do something about this place, like get rid of it, because that in effect would ideally get rid of all the riffraff that came along with it. He shined the light in the store.

A shadow dashed through the beam and quickly vanished.

He scratched his head.

He went into the store to see what was going on. The light scanned a row of T-shirts suspended high up on a black wall, and stopped on a Green Day shirt. John had brought his son, Nick, to see Green Day live in concert for Nick's twelfth birthday, a year prior to the accident. Green Day had been Nick's favorite band. John shook the memory out of his head and willed himself to focus on the present, instead of getting dragged into the past. If policing had taught him anything, it was to prepare for any and every possibility, and right now it was important he didn't lose it, because one wrong move could cost him his life.

He continued through the store and came to a door in the back. He holstered both the flashlight and the gun and unclipped from his belt a large key ring looped through a multitude of keys. He scanned the set of keys for the correct one, found it, and unlocked the door.

13

He entered a dark, narrow passage with blue walls and an orange floor, leading him lower into the ground as he followed it all the way to the end, and man, was it a long descent. The corridor just kept going and going and going, until it stopped at a blue steel door. He tried the handle, but it was hopeless, for he had never ventured to this stretch of the mall before and, scanning the large key ring, couldn't find the correct key for the door.

He tried the handle one more time, hoping to jiggle the lock loose, when a *ding*ing sound like that of a cowbell occurred, and, startled by the sound, he jumped back. He rubbed his chin for a moment, deciding his next move, before hitting the door with his heel, a *thud*ding impact, the door rattling, but it still wouldn't budge. He tried again, and the vibration from the impact shot through his leg, a stinging sensation nestling in his groin. He was baffled. He decided that, just like the door, the situation was hopeless, and turned around to ascend back to where he had come.

He went up, and up, and up, and up, and up. The narrow corridor just kept going and going, and his ascent seemed much longer than his descent. His breathing became much shallower as he hiked up the hallway. He didn't remember delving this far in on his way down. It had been a long descent, sure. But not quite as long as this. He stopped for a moment, panting and trying to catch his breath. Ever since he'd left the Force, exercise had been a low priority, and currently he was cursing himself for not taking better care of his health.

The remainder of his climb seemed an entire mile before he came to a blue brick wall, the door through which he'd come seeming to have disappeared. The light weaved all around, searching for an exit, as panic set in. His heart *thump-thump*ed inside his chest, the pounding so loud he could hear it in his head, and he could feel sweat beading on his skin and streaming down his face. He ran a hand through his moist hair, then wiped his damped palms on his pants. For the first time in two months John contemplated a drink. He figured that a couple shots of whiskey would give him the answers. Just a couple. Three, he knew, would do the trick more effectively, though. Or maybe even four. No, no, no, that wasn't right at all. Five would definitely do the trick. He knew that for sure.

No, that wasn't right, either. Three months had gone by without him having to drink. Think, John. Think, think, think, he repeated as he paced up and down the path. Think!!! There was a way out; there had to be. His AA sponsor had always told him that. Had always said, "Things will always work themselves out one way or another." But he couldn't fathom any future at present. All he could think of was the hopelessness of the situation. He'd crossed through a doorway and into a hallway and had followed the hall to a locked steel door. Then had turned around and ascended back to the doorway through which he'd come, though the door had mysteriously vanished and now John was trapped in this creepy corridor, with no escape whatsoever.

Things will always work themselves out one way or another, he reminded himself. His heart picked up its pace, beating even faster now. He could die of starvation. What was he to do?

That was it; that was the answer he was looking for. His AA sponsor would guide him out, somehow. He took out his cellphone and flipped it open. He only had one solitary bar of service.

John....

He could sense someone—or something—calling his name. It came so suddenly that he accidentally squeezed off a shot, the darkness sparking with a bright flash and a reverberating *bang!*, followed by a relentless ringing in his ears.

John Karr….

He turned, and the light rounded the wall in a wave.

Then on blinked a bright light directly above him. He whipped around, gun at ready, just to watch a procession of fluorescent lights, one after another, flash on, travelling all the way down the hall, almost as if to say, *come hither!*, paving a path for John to go down.

In a panic he tried his cellphone with its dwindling service and waited and waited for a ringtone. But it never came. Time ticked away as he waited.

He snapped his phone shut, and gulped down the knot lodged in his throat.

John, come here. I've got something to show you.

He started after the line of lights illuminating the trail, with a faint buzz that sounded like the inside of a beehive. His pace steadily sped up as he went down, ignoring the pestering pressure of being short of breath.

He followed the succession of fluorescent lights all the way until the hallway ran out and he was stopped at the door that had been locked the last time he had checked. He tried the door again, yanking the handle this way and that, but it was still locked. He continued to wriggle the handle, the lock jingling inside the door, but it was no use.

He stopped, resting his hands on his hips.

Get a grip on yourself, John.

Security Guard Gothic

"Hello?"

Don't lose it, John.

"Who said that?"

John Karr, it's me. Don't you remember me?

He hadn't heard anything; the hallway was absolutely silent. All he was left with were his own thoughts, and they danced through his head as if they weren't his own, as if someone else had tapped into his stream-of-conscious. Who did he not remember? Or moreover, what the hell was going on? He had to find out.

He tried the door again, wriggling the handle.

Hahahahaha!!! Giddy childish laughter rolled through his mind.

He released the handle then and fell into deep thought.

It came to him at once and he took a step back, pointed the gun down at a slight angle, steadied his hands by taking deep, calming breaths, and finally squeezed the trigger. The shot tore the handle from the door, leaving only a hole in its wake.

With the barrel of the gun pressed flush to the door, he slowly and cautiously pushed the door open. As he did this, he heard a sudden *thump*—and he jumped, whirled around toward where it had come—and then another, come from behind, and the lights were rapidly shutting off, one after another, the darkness coming toward him until he was engulfed in it.

He cautiously crept through the doorway, fearful. He shined the light in front of him and found that he was in a dungeon of some sort, the walls made of metal, and the air was hot. Really hot. Like a boiler room.

"John Karr." A barely audible whisper, still unrecognizable.

"John Karr." A little louder this time, but not by much. *Hahahahaha!!!*

"John Karr." This time, he heard it clearly, and the voice sounded frightfully familiar, like someone from the past, someone he had cared tremendously about, someone he had deeply loved, someone who had left a permanent impression on his heart.

Nick!

The voice belonged to Nick.

"That's right, John, it's me," the voice said and echoed off the metallic walls.

"N-N-N-Nick." He struggled to say it, fright biting down hard on his tongue.

"You killed me, John."

"B-b-but-but it was an a-a-accident," he said, and felt the first tear roll down his face, and then another on the other side.

"JOOOOOOHN!!!"

The lights flashed on above him, and he was standing in the center of a circle made up of people, all wearing red robes that covered their feet and touched the floor, with hoods flipped over their heads.

The circle was closed in around him and any resemblance to the corridor through which he'd come had disappeared behind these strange … ?

He scanned the room, walking in panicked circles, searching for an escape route as the circle came closer, getting smaller around him, the red robes seeming to float. John looked above him, and the ceiling was light-pink, with no way out … and no way in. He started firing maniacally at these freaks, and each one stirred a bit when the bullet hit, but none of them went down.

When he was out of bullets, he chucked the gun at one of them, and the thing jerked its head out of the way with unreal speed, the gun flying and spiraling past. There sounded a *clank* and a *clatter* when the gun hit the wall behind them. He then felt like vomiting, the fear was so great. He continued turning in circles as they continued closing in, and then he did vomit, bending over and releasing a blend of chewed Big Mac and Red Bull.

He dropped to his knees, hopelessness and guilt and regret getting the better of him as these creeps moved in for the kill. When they were as close as they could get without trampling him, they pounced like a pack of hungry wolves attacking one lone sheep, ripping him apart, limb by limb, and slashing up his skin with their long, sharp claw-like fingernails. On his knees John covered his face and screamed in pain, feeling each piece of flesh ripped away and each limb plucked right from the rest of his body as shock took over and numbness soothed the fresh wounds.

He let out one final horrifying cry …

… everything slowing to a stop …

It was dark on the drive home, and the stars shined like glitter in the night sky. The crescent-shaped moon looked like a glowing hole in the black canvas. Traffic was bustling, cars drifting by on the left of John and his family, who all rode buckled in to the soft seats in their brand-new Volkswagen. John sat behind the wheel, with Susan in the passenger seat, Nick in the back, and one glance in the rearview mirror showed John that taking Nick to Dave and Busters for his birthday had worked out successfully, his son's smile beaming with exuberance as he stared out the window with wide, enquiring eyes.

A mile ahead up the highway an eighteen-wheeler was descending the onramp. As it went down in an arc formation, the Karr family rode in the farthest right lane, just left of the breakdown lane, for their exit was approaching. They were getting closer to the truck.

One mile later they were passing the long truck that was still riding in the breakdown lane and drifting leftward, inching closer to the Volkswagen.

John didn't notice how close the truck was getting.

Susan didn't notice, either.

Nick noticed but was too late, because the truck tore the passenger-side door right off and shoved the car into the path of an oncoming van which hit them head-on. The Volkswagen spun out of control, screeching as the tires skidded sideways. Then it flipped and sparks flickered up from under the rooftop as it slid to a screeching stop, John and Nick each having hit their head so hard they were knocked out cold.

... and John could remember now, the memory playing in his head as though it were happening at present ...

In the hospital a couple of months later, after coming out of a coma, John learned that Susan had been ripped right out of her seat before the van had even hit them. She had passed away that night, and so had Nick. He had died, the doctor told John, right here in the hospital from a concussion caused by the crash.

It came back to him as a hand slashed at his neck and crisp claws ripped out his throat. He groped at the hole and struggled to breathe, his head smacking the ground as he went down.

——and then there was a sudden bright flash that vaporized all the attacking beings——for only a moment; the light absorbing the things for only an instant—and then the blast of light blinked out and everything was frozen still, the red-robed creatures stopping mid-slash as the seemingly razor-sharp spikes protruding from their fingertips created thin streaks in the air. John was horrified, more frightened than he'd ever been in all his life, and in their frozen state he could make out their long, pointed noses and big, round bug-like eyes and the trimmed layer of gray fur covering their faces. He could see the thin, furry tails frozen behind them in fluid, curving shapes, coiling with the momentum of their bodyweight bringing down their spiked fingernails.

"Jooohhn," a voice cooed softly. "Jooohhn." He recognized the voice almost immediately; it was that of his dead wife, soft and sweet with a heart-startling spice woven in. "Jooohhn."

"Susan," John said, touching the hole in his neck, checking his fingertips, and he saw the smudged black blood. He winced at the sight. "Susan," he cried, knowing his time had come, that this was it, he was in heaven. Heavy sobs arose from John's dying form. "Susan," he balled, wiping the tears from his eyes.

"Jooohhn," she said, and she sounded like an angel.

She appeared, floating through the frozen onslaught of crea-tures—*floating!* She was floating, wearing the same red robe, and as she came closer he could make out her long, pointed nose and big bug-eyes and gray fury face. The light in the dungeon started to fade into a reddish yellow, like searing hot flames.

She neared him, and he saw the light in her eyes, the flickering something that seemed to become more visible as she stopped be-fore him, and what he saw in her eyes were fires, a single flame licking at each socket. Thick, gray billows of smoke rushed out the bottom of her robe and wafted up into the air, making John squint.

"You killed me," she said, jabbing downward at him with her pointer finger.

"It was an a-a-accident."

The lights flickered to darkness—at which point images of Nick's laughing face flooded his mind—and then a burst of bright light erased all traces of the black that had encompassed the room only moments ago, John's thoughts haunted with that eerie image of his son.

"It was an a-a-accident."

Nick was in his head now. Nick was laughing in his head, the laughter loud and maddening. Nick was mocking him, that's what he was doing: mocking him and laughing at the misery imposed upon his own father. This was funny to Nick, funny and deserving—yes, quite deserving.

"You were drunk, John," Susan said. "How could you possibly say it was an accident? I would always scorn you for your senseless drunk-driving excursions. But you never listened, John, you never listened."

Nick was laughing menacingly, he was guffawing and spitting out enjoyment, he was happy, so very happy, the first time John had seen him happy since that horrible night. In fact, this was the first time he'd seen Nick at all since....

"Please," he cried out. "P-please, make it sss-stop."

"I'm not doing anything, John."

"P-please."

Suddenly the laughter ceased.

"JOOOOOOHN!!!"—Nick's voice.

"Jooohhn"—Susan's voice.

"Hahahahaha!!!"—Nick's voice.

Security Guard Gothic

"Hahaha!"—Susan's voice. "Jooohhn. Listen to me, John."

"If I could rewind time and do it all over again, I would." He was crying, his head buried in his hands. "Just make it stop!" He sniffled. "P-please, make it stop."

"Okay," Susan said. "As you wish."

As the images of Nick faded from his mind and the floating Susan faded into the background, time resumed and he felt a sharp pressure tearing into his shin. A brief spasm flashed through his whole body, all the way from his head to his toes, and he flipped over onto his back and saw one of the creatures gnawing on his leg. The tremors soon subsided, and a dull numbness overtook his nervous system. He watched as a crisp claw slashed through his stomach and scooped up a handful of flesh. He watched himself get eaten alive, watched the horror, the horrific things feeding on him like a flock of ravens swarming a dead carcass, the revolting sight causing his vision to blur, causing his conscious to blacken, to fade into nothing, his mind shutting off like a bedside lamp at bedtime, darkness overtaking his thoughts, his head heavy with emptiness. He released a single childish scream.

.......................*STOP*

Time almost seemed to rewind.

<<< Everything *P--L--A--Y--ed* backwards.

——the red-robed creatures backing away ...

Three

years

earlier

John tossed his keys to his wife and said, "Maybe you should drive. I'm kind of drunk."

"But," Susan said, "you never let me drive. Is everything all right?"

"Yeah," he said, ducking his head beneath the roof and settling down in the passenger seat.

They drove home, and Susan slowed down the Volkswagen to let in the truck. After the truck veered in front of them, John swiveled his head and stared at his son in the back, Nick, whose smile brought John a feeling of joy.

In the Van
Which Was Soaring Down the Freeway

In the van, which was soaring down the freeway, in the fastest lane, there were six teenagers, ranging from the ages 14 to 20—OK, I guess one, the oldest, was out of his teens. His name was Terry; and then there was Terry's younger sister, Marla; and Marla's boyfriend, Ricky; and then the driver, who they called Kevin; and finally the hitchhiking twins from Boston, Breanna and Hunter, who had grown up in Rutland, Vermont, and had come back for a wake, and afterwards they went barhopping and found the town was lame, so they decided to hitchhike to Burlington when the van, going the other way, swerved to the left and shuddered over the yellow line and pulled to a haphazard stop on the side of the highway. The sliding door opened with a bang, and thick billows of smoke, which clearly smelt of pot, poured out the opening, and through the smoke screen emerged Ricky, who hopped out and gestured the siblings in. Breanna entered first, then Hunter who was behind her, and as he climbed in Terry bumped his shoulder going out and bent and vomited in the brush lining the edge of the street.

In the van Ricky introduced them to his girlfriend, Marla, and in the front Kevin turned his head toward the back and he said yo and told them his name. What were they doing out here this late at night? he asked the twins. Breanna told them the story, told them how they'd come from Rutland, which was a bust, and were now heading to Burlington. So Ricky asked if they were indeed looking for thrills, for kicks, shits, and giggles, and Hunter nodded yes and said of course they were. And a fat blunt appeared in Hunter's face. He took it from Marla's grasp and he took a toke and pulled it in and held the smoke down and when he passed it off to Breanna, Terry entered the van and slammed the door shut.

The van rumbled to a start and eased out into the street and then took off.

For Breanna and Hunter, it wasn't long before things started feeling fuzzy, like the dots, the polkadots, or whatever you wanna call those things, flashing and flickering in front of Hunter's eyes like a disco light, and he attempted to bat them away like flies with his open hand. This act made Ricky laugh, and he nudged the shoulder of his girlfriend who was taking her turn on the blunt. The nudge startled her a bit and she ripped the blunt from her mouth, diverted her eyes to her boyfriend, and then followed the line of his head gesture to where Hunter was swatting at the air with his hand, a phantom hand following its tread like a tail, and Marla laughed. Breanna didn't notice her brother's foolish behavior, for she had her own set of problems—she was walking toward the light, walking to heaven, and the light was so bright she couldn't see the passengers in the van anymore. Oh yeah, that's right, she was in a van, and in that moment the light sizzled out and someone slapped her hard in the face, her head whipping around and to the side, and she peered deep into her brother's apologetic eyes, could see his soul, the soul of someone who had just slapped her.

Then the van swerved and the horn howled and Hunter rolled over onto Marla, Breanna onto Ricky, while Terry was still standing, taking a hit, his back to the wall, which was without a doubt what had kept him right-side up.

As the twins got their bearings back, Breanna still irritated by the slap to her face, but willing to forgive because it was her brother for krissake, the couple on the floor plus Terry who was standing were all laughing and laughing, finding something funny, and they wouldn't stop, so Hunter rubbed his head, wondering what was so funny, and then opened his mouth to speak but his sister beat him to it and asked rather curtly what was the deal?

The weed, Ricky laughed.

It was laced with PCP, Marla added, laughing too.

Only the thing was, how the laughing couple had said it was slow and low, like a deep, droning voice, like if you put your tape player on slow, that was how they spoke it, and now the siblings were scared and mad for being betrayed like that, but then again they were never told but just assumed the weed was clean, and they smoked it without question, and as Ricky explained that was the case and Marla's laughter played in the background like a manic laugh track and Kevin continued to drive, taking a hit as he did so, and Terry, well, Terry was being Terry, Breanna and Hunter continued to be angry and they shouted, shouted, shouted, but what were they gonna do about it now, anyway? Terry challenged.

He puffed out his chest and paced the center of the van and Hunter's complaining retreated but even so Breanna poked a finger out and continued to shout.

But a sudden backhanded slap took care of that right away. She looked at Terry, the man who'd done it to her, and said why did everybody keep hitting her? The whole van began cracking up, including Hunter, who was too scared not to laugh. Well, Breanna was not laughing, for she was just so damned mad. Hunter gave her a slight nudge and said hey, sis, ease up a bit.

Something about the genuine calm in her brother's voice, or just the sheer fact that she wasn't alone, that her brother was here too, made her ease up on the anger she felt, the anger of being slapped around by men—ooooh, how she hated that—and the anger of being given PCP without being informed—she didn't know how she felt about that, because she would never have expected it to happen, not to her, but it had in fact happened and then she'd gotten slapped twice, once by her brother which was okay to an extent, but Terry had slapped her too, and suddenly the anger was back, she was so mad.

Let me out of here! she demanded, pumping a pissed-off fist in the air. Stop the van! Kevin's head whirled and he was facing the back and for the first time his eyes connected with Breanna's, and he said no dice. He said they don't stop, not now, not then, not ever, but only when the sun comes out and the morning light casts shadows on the ground, and anyway has that even happened yet? No it hasn't. So why doesn't she shut the fuck up and smoke some more. She did shut up, although she didn't smoke anymore. Her brother too was horrified, and when the van rolled into the gas station lot and the three passengers in the back—Ricky, Marla, and

In the Van

Terry—pulled out big heaving guns and put masks of dead poets on over their faces and threw open the door, he thought about running, thought about it, but then saw the gun trained on him and his sister, Kevin holding it steady, Hunter thinking this was how it ended, and both twins' jaws dropped, they were stunned.

Don't even think about it, Kevin said behind the handgun he held expertly and kept aimed at the twins. If they tried anything, he warned, he would put a bullet through the back of their heads. Then he laughed, and said, Or he'd stick the gun up both their butts and the bullet would rip through their guts and they'd fall flat in the gas station lot as the van veered out and took off.

Then in through the door came the three dead poets with a fifth man in tow, the store clerk, Hunter supposed, who had a dark stain over his crotch and smelt like piss and he was all gross and freckly, Breanna observed, and then the van veered out of the gas station lot and the kid screamed as it cut right and the whole van quaked.

Breanna grimaced when she saw the liquid pooling by the kid's right leg, dripping out of his pants, although Hunter didn't notice it himself, and instantly his own bladder let go too, only moderately, and he glanced down at his pants feeling ashamed of himself but there were no urine stains there, and although you think he'd be relieved, he wasn't at all because these big guns, the biggest handguns he'd ever seen, were cocked and loaded and could take him out with only one shot.

What was this young kid doing here? Breanna wanted to know and practically snapped at the inhabitants of this van, but Hunter grasped her arm lightly and chided her to just let it go. Let it go? she spoke unsurely to her brother, for when did his balls fall off?

Her brother was never a wimp; in fact, Breanna had always admired his courage, his bravery, the fact that he would never back down. But now was different, as these guys and one girl who'd picked them up were carrying guns and holding a store clerk hostage for reasons unknown to her. A slight nod of her head signaled to her brother that she was scared, and she waved the PCP-laced smoke out of her face. Can't believe they're still smoking that shit, she whispered to her brother. Just play it cool, he suggested, play it cool. This would be over soon, and it wasn't worth losing an eye. But what about the kid? she said, clearly worried. What about him? her brother said, bashfully. There was nothing they could do. He was about to say more, to assure his sister that they would get out of here in one piece, when, suddenly, a sharp metallic sound stole his attention, and when he craned his neck that way he found himself looking down the barrel of Ricky's gun. Speak up, he ordered. No secrets allowed. Breanna gulped and gave Hunter's arm a tug.

Hunter looked at his sister, then back at the gun; then at Ricky, whose face was glazed over with a fierce stare; then at Marla, who was taking a toke from the blunt, and then passing it off to the kid. What was his name? Marla asked him. He didn't speak, though. He just looked at Breanna who was swiveling her head back and forth to tell the kid not to hit it. Marla repeated herself, and the kid looked back at her and flinched when she raised the gun overhead and moved to bring it down, just hit him with the butt of it, but the kid spit out, James. His name was James, he informed them, passing the blunt to Terry. But Terry held out his hands and shook his head, and so the kid tried handing it off to Ricky then Marla, then Breanna and Hunter, but nobody wanted it, and

In the Van

Ricky said, Take a hit. The kid's head weaved. He looked like a frightened pig. Take a hit, Terry said. Take a hit, came from Marla next. Take a hit, they all sang together. Breanna went to save the kid, to take the blunt from him, but the muzzle of a gun told her not to. Her hands retreated to her sides.

Finally the kid brought the blunt to his lips, but when the van swerved, he dropped it on the floor. The van rumbled and then stopped.

Terry threw open the door and grabbed James on his way out. With his gun Terry led James through the field, down a hill, with Breanna and Hunter on their heels, while three handguns were poking them in the backs and directing them to keep on going, to follow James and Terry, and they did, they went, they staggered, the PCP still controlling their minds, with dots appearing in Hunter's sight and a bright light in Breanna's. They went forward, and could hear Kevin, Ricky, and Marla laughing at their rears, shamelessly like a bunch of hyenas. Hunter looked up at the sky, and there were a ton of stars up there; in spite of everything to-night, he had to admit the sight was rather beautiful, and he let his sister know, and she took a gander upward and for once smiled, at the sight, and the expression on her face assured Hunter that he wasn't just seeing the stars, that it wasn't just an effect of the PCP, although some of the stars Breanna herself couldn't see, because some of them were indeed just a direct effect of the PCP. Which ones? Hunter would never know, and he wasn't about to ask, because the sight was pretty and that was all there was to it.

They came to a line of trees and were led to a narrow path that cut through the center, and looking down the trail Hunter couldn't see a thing, nor could his sister who was frozen at the start of the trail, frozen solid and too scared to move. Kevin nudged her with his pistol, but even so she remained frozen. He pushed her harder, and Hunter extended his hand to hers, and together, hand and hand, they walked along the dark path, the wind swooshing loudly through the trees, and the branches scraping together like grinding teeth, the leaves flittering about. It sounded like the trail was haunted, like ghouls were swooping through the woods.

They continued through the path, hands still clutched between them, and little slants of moonlight managed to break through the gaps and sprinkle the ground with fluorescent cobwebs.

There was a clearing up ahead, where James stood by himself shaking in the cold air and probably due to his frightened nerves, too. He looked quite unhappy, his face contorted into a scowl, and his shirt was torn, a slash that ran from his right shoulder down to his chest at an angle and stopped halfway down his left side, and a flap hung over his stomach, and in the torn section you could see he wore a black thermal beneath his work shirt. His nose was bloodied like he'd been punched there, and his lip was split in the middle, with a line of blood showing where exactly the lip parted, and he just looked so cold and frightened standing there on his own. Hunter ditched his captors and darted to where James stood shivering, his teeth thrashing inside his mouth, the sound loud enough for Hunter to hear when he reached him and asked if he was okay. It was then when Terry came back, his gun tilted and trained on Hunter, who when seeing the deadly weapon stepped back from James as Terry stepped closer, and Hunter kept going backwards.

When Terry reached where Hunter had been standing in front of James, he ground his fist into James's gut. James folded when

In the Van

the fist connected, and he flopped down on his knees and bowed his head in defeat, and Terry prodded him in the head with the gun to get up, now. James stood reluctantly, and when he was fully on his feet, Terry reeled in the gun and sent it backhandedly into James's mouth. The hit forced his face to the side, and the other three holding guns started cackling in laughter, but Breanna and Hunter weren't amused at all, and Hunter wanted to protest this, wanted to stop it and save the kid, being that he was a brave one, but Breanna's soft touch told him he shouldn't. She rubbed his hand with her thumb and pointer finger, keeping him calm and cool, and each twin's eyes met with the other's, and Breanna stared into her brother's eyes as Hunter stared into his sister's, and their heads sat motionless on their necks, facing the side, facing each other, and they were making a plan to escape, via eye contact. The others didn't notice this because they were too busy laughing as Terry pummeled James with the butt of his handgun, slap after slap after slap. Breanna and Hunter didn't watch his beating, but heard the sound of the gun coming down on him, the sound of the butt connecting, and the sound of him yelping for help, screaming for his mother to come save and protect him—*Mommy!, Mommy!, Mommy!*—and his pained cries were maddening, neither Breanna nor Hunter knowing how the rest could take it, how they could find it so funny. Must be the PCP, was what Breanna figured, still staring into her brother's eyes. Then there came the loudest sound of all, a deafening bang, which in a way forced the twins to look, and when they did, they saw James falling backwards, flat like a Domino, and flopping hard on the dirt, his head hitting the ground last with a loud crack, and smoke was trailing up from the muzzle of Terry's handgun which he held pointed straight ahead.

35

Hunter gasped and a second later Breanna screamed, and soon the two of them broke loose from the others' grasps and ran to James to see if he was okay. But immediately they were flanked by the other three holding guns and Terry came from the front and cut them off. Breanna and Hunter stopped where they were, and Terry ordered them to lug James's body back to the van or else he would force the two of them to fuck over there—he pointed with his pistol—on the grass. Now, grab his body, Terry demanded, and haul him back to the van, and they did, Breanna lifting his feet and Hunter his head, and they carried him while Ricky and Marla, holding hands, walked in the rear, their guns aimed and ready, and Kevin and Terry led the way, turning every now and then to point their guns at the twins who had sickened expressions on their faces.

They had to get away somehow, Breanna whispered to her brother. But he was already aware of this and let his sister know, but he didn't know how they would, was what he said to her, and her head turned in disapproval, a slow and steady movement, weaving from one side to another, at a slant that kept her facing down at her feet. She was just so ashamed of herself right now. She would never let herself live this down.

They emerged from the path and stalked through the grass and up the hill and came to the van, and Terry swung the backdoor wide open and told them to prop the body there, and they did, just set him on his side. Waving their guns as though directing airplanes on the runway, they motioned for the twins to enter through the side door, which Terry pulled open, and the frightened twins walked past him into the van and found seats on the floor, and Hunter's knees stuck up, his feet flush with the floor, and he hugged them tight to his chest as his sister held on to his side, her arms wrapped around his neck, and she was shuddering, her chest heaving hard, and Hunter was worried sick and he started coughing and gagging himself.

This was how it ended, Hunter said to himself, nervously rocking back and forth on his butt, as his sister held on to him as though he were a lifesaver and if she let go, she would drown. She didn't want to drown, not now, not tonight; she didn't want to go out without a fight, and then Ricky entered the van through the side door, and Marla was right behind him, and Terry came in next and shut the door and looked at the twins and said are they okay? The moment Terry had said it Breanna began to weep, quietly, and her brother's face shown with worry, and Terry called them both sensitive when the front door opened and Kevin sidled in, turned on the engine, put the van in drive, and steered it out into the street, and the speed of it increased immensely as the van glided along.

Hunter looked at Breanna and her teary eyes made his stomach do somersaults, cartwheels, backflips; made his heart clench, and he looked away and his eyes met Terry's eyes, and it seemed Terry had been staring this whole time at Hunter, with a sickeningly hungry facial expression. Hunter cringed when he saw Terry's tongue come out of his mouth and run along the edge of his bottom lip. What did he want? Hunter queried, and Terry said nothing. C'mon, man, what the hell did he want? Terry lifted a stiff pointer finger straight up in the air and brought it down slow and steady, and finally said he didn't know why he was staring like that, didn't even realize it, and for once even apologized, which was completely unexpected, and Hunter glanced at the body and then back up at Terry, then at his sister who sat huddled up beside him, and then at Terry again and said he forgave him, which was an outright lie, though Hunter had to admit that having Terry stare at him was the least of his problems, and then came three clacks, and Hunter craned his neck toward the sound and Ricky was busy bashing two handguns together, with more clacks coming from the impact, and all the while Marla was laughing for some odd reason. She was laughing and clapping and cheering him on. Breanna was so frightened, as was her brother, for what if one of the guns went off in the van? and suddenly one did, a bang louder than the one that had killed James, and the shot punctured a jagged hole in the roof. Everyone was laughing now, except Breanna and Hunter, and Breanna clutched her brother even tighter while Hunter was chanting in his head that he could escape, he was stronger than them, he was tougher, he had more balls, and he could do it.

He asked Ricky if he could see one of the guns. Ricky looked at him curiously, and Marla told Ricky it was a mistake to let him see one, and Terry's head was shaking no, no, no, and so Ricky handed Hunter a gun, Marla's handgun, and Hunter looked at it, observed it, studied it, for he had never held one before, and then stuck it against the side of Ricky's head. Marla gasped and Terry took his own gun and pointed it at Hunter as Breanna said what was he doing? What was he thinking?

He would blow his fuckin head off, Hunter warned. Terry, put down the fuckin gun. Terry smiled a smile so menacing that the sight of it made Hunter shudder, and the gun in Terry's grip panned just an inch to point at Ricky, and Terry's smile grew even wider. Do it, then, Terry said, pointing his pistol at Ricky's chest. C'mon, man, do it! The sudden burst of bravery that Hunter had

In the Van

felt faded rather quickly, and instantly a bullet ripped out of Terry's gun and tore into Ricky's chest. Terry was still smiling, staring challengingly into Hunter's eyes, as if to convey a message, and Hunter, still pressing the gun against the side of Ricky's head, was completely stunned by what Terry had done, and Breanna's gaze was wavering from Hunter to Ricky to Hunter to Ricky.

Terry! Marla finally gasped.

Kevin glanced in the back and began laughing.

Hunter's gaze remained on Ricky's sunken head.

Breanna said, Do something!

Hunter retracted the gun and turned and pressed it against the side of Marla's head, and Terry realigned his gun with Hunter, who said he was dead serious. If Terry didn't hand over his gun, Hunter would blow Marla's head clean off.

Terry lowered his gun and the van swerved and Hunter told Kevin to stop the van now. But Kevin only turned his head toward the back and he said no dice, and then the van started speeding up rapidly, Kevin laughing in the driver's seat. Hunter lifted the gun from Marla's head, and she sighed too soon, because right away he belted her with the butt of the gun and said stop the van. Marla screamed as the gun hit her in the head a second time, but after a third time she was silenced and kinda resembled Ricky. Hunter pressed the gun to the side of her head and said he wasn't going to say it again, stop the van. Kevin looked in the back and Hunter could see the fear on his face, and Breanna's head was shaking in disapproval, and Terry said OK, stop the van. Not looking at the road, eyes still focused on the passengers in the back, Kevin shook his head no as the van cut across the highway and hit a rut and bounced and landed on the grass and rolled past the edge of a small lake, before Kevin turned and stomped on the brake. The van jerked to a sudden stop.

The momentum surged through the van like an electroshock, everyone snapping forward and then back, and Terry's gun skittered across the floor and smacked against the backdoor. Hunter lunged at it, grabbed it, and Terry was right behind him, diving on top of Hunter's back. On the floor of the van they wrestled for control of the gun, rolling around and throwing punches— Hunter's clenched fist flying into Terry's face, Terry's bony knee going up into Hunter's groin, Hunter's hard head flinging forward and striking the bridge of Terry's nose for the final blow—and as Terry reached up and grabbed his swollen face, Hunter gained control of the gun and aimed it at Terry, who didn't know until he lowered his hands from his face and saw he was looking straight down the barrel, and Hunter told him to open the door, now. Terry opened it and stepped outside. Breanna exited next. Hunter ordered Kevin to hand over his gun too, and he did. Hunter checked to make sure the safety was on, then stuffed it in his pants and, with one pistol pointed at Marla and the other pointed at Terry, left the van and slammed the door shut. He gave his sister one of the guns, the one in his left hand, and the two of them walked toward Terry who took baby-steps backwards.

Then the front door opened and shut. Hunter turned suddenly. Something slammed into his ankle, which twisted, and he dropped to a knee. He looked up at his sister who fumbled with the trigger, and instantly a fist hit him in the eye. The side of his face smacked the street which scraped a couple stinging slashes deep into his cheek. He pushed himself up and Kevin was standing behind Breanna, holding a gun to the back of her head. Hand over both guns, Terry said. He held out his hand and curled his fingers back and forth. Hunter handed him both guns and Marla was already holding the one Breanna had, and Hunter was directed to stand and the twins were led down a dip, with a red light seeping into the black sky overhead and a golden circle bobbing up from behind the hills, with cars buzzing by on the street, the first wave of drivers on their way to work.

Terry ordered them to drop to their knees and put their hands behind their heads, and of course they obeyed, without a question, and the sound of tires swishing on the street and coming to a stop came from the top of the hill. Shit, Kevin said. Go check on it, Terry said. Kevin started to climb the hill, his gun held steady out in front.

Then, red and blue lights splashed down the hill, highlighting the captors and their hostages, and Kevin turned and shouted cops! Fear struck Terry's face, and he uttered run!!! In a tight-knit group they all scurried off into the woods, including Breanna and Hunter, with guns forcing them forward, and Hunter in a split decision kicked Terry between the legs with as much raw might as he could muster, and Terry stumbled and fumbled with the gun which rolled out of his grasp and kept going on the grass, and Hunter scooped it up, leveled it with Terry who was hopping around in agony, holding his wounded groin, and said don't move! Everybody froze then, at the sound of his command, and scanning the scene real quick he jumped up and brought the butt down hard on Terry's head, which went crashing into the grass with a dull thud.

Hunter panned the weapon in his hand, whirling to point it at each and every one of them, but when he heard the footsteps coming nearer and saw the flashlight beam cutting through the dimness, he turned to Breanna and told her to run. The twins ran, they darted through the slight light that was getting brighter, they dodged trees that hurtled toward them like arrows, with a stampede of feet right at their rear, and they kept on going, even though their breathing only got heavier and harder to maintain. They reached an opening and came out on a side street, and by that point it was fully morning, the dark sky now lit up bright, and they stopped at the edge of the woods marveling at the sight.

The PCP was fully out of their systems too.

Hunter glanced behind him, and the rest were nowhere to be found, nor were any cops, and the two of them cut a right back on the highway and strolled along the side of the street. When a different van came soaring by from behind them, Breanna stuffed her hands in her pockets as Hunter craned his neck to watch it pass, with the sharp swishing sound of tires gliding on the asphalt, and the twins didn't speak about what had happened back there as they walked away holding hands, into the magnificently bright sunlight, without plans.

Nefarious Endeavor #1

Late one Friday night Paula and Andy were walking along Main Street, with a slight drizzle overhead. The rain clattered against the umbrella Andy held in his hand. Cars buzzed by, kicking up water from under the tires. They passed a man in a dark trench coat also holding up an umbrella.

Earlier on, Andy had taken Paula to TGI Fridays, where they had a blast, and laughed at all the karaoke performances—the old Japanese man who couldn't dance and whose voice stank; the even older man with a harmonica who really got into the music, shaking his rump and bumping his head; the fat younger drunk whose words slurred and who looked like he was going to croak any minute (Paula hoped he would); the young girl who seemed way to young to be there; the married couple singing together a lame love song; and of course the big-breasted old lady who swayed from side to side, making her boobs jiggle like Jello. This, and more.

Presently Paula and Andy had a slight swagger in their step, but managed to stay grounded by leaning in close to each other. Paula was so happy with how Andy treated her. She never thought she'd meet a guy like him. The man of her dreams.

She was excited too, for Andy had promised her a surprise back at the car. A wedding ring, maybe. She hoped. She was going to marry this man and be the mother of his children.

She wanted four, because she never had any brothers and sisters of her own and always wished she had. So she wouldn't deny her own children the gift of siblings.

The rain was beginning to ebb, and when it fully cleared, Andy lowered and folded the umbrella. The sound of moving traffic swishing through the puddles on the street died off too and the summer heat rose to a sweltering temp, Paula starting to feel a little disgusted when sweat streamed under her raincoat.

She quickly removed it and handed it to Andy, who had no problem holding onto it and his own heavy raincoat too.

They turned down the side street where the car was parked, and when they approached the glistening red Jaguar, Paula's lights flickered out and she dropped to the ground, hitting her head on the curb.

Andy saw her collapse, but rather than wonder what had happened, he reached in his pocket and fetched a cigarette, his moonlit shadow blanketing her fallen body as he pulled smoke into his lungs, craning his neck to see Todd standing behind him, also smoking a cigarette.

Their eyes met, and they stood there silently for a while finishing up their cigarettes, then snuffed the smoldering butts into the pavement and bent down to pick up Paula. She didn't weigh too much, and it would have really only taken one person to pick her up and store her in the trunk, but since the two of them were already there they figured the more the merrier.

Andy thrust down on the trunk, turned to Todd and locked eyes. As Todd entered the passenger side Andy entered the driver side, then maneuvered the Jaguar into the street and drove away slow enough so as not to draw any attention as they vanished with Paula in the back.

Don't Look in the Trunk!

Officer Henry Brown was horrified of what he might find in that trunk. He stared at it, and the thing seemed to be taunting him. He heard something come from inside, and he wondered what it was. It sounded like a thud and a thump and a thunk, all mixed together and played at once.

"Henry!"

He looked up then and saw his partner, Officer Karl Buttkiss, standing by the suspect, who'd claimed his name was Mort Ellis, but they had no way of being sure. Ellis had a valid ID, that they knew. But he could have lied. He could have, nobody knew for sure.

"Henry," Buttkiss said.

"Yeah?" Brown replied.

"What's in the trunk?"

A look of fright showed in the suspect's eyes. Ellis, Brown could tell, was afraid of what might come if Brown looked in the trunk.

Brown walked back to Buttkiss and said, "I think he's telling the truth."

Brown then looked in Ellis's eyes, which were dashing from side to side.

Brown's gaze slid down the length of the car and stopped on the passenger in the back. His name was Derek Robinson, Ellis had claimed, and Robinson sat up straight in the car, but stared out the window through the corner of his eye. He was sweating too; he was nervous, Brown knew.

Buttkiss shined the flashlight in Ellis's eyes again, and the brown dots darted out of the way. His eyes were ridden with blood, and his pupils were big and round. He was clearly high.

On what? Brown wondered as he analyzed Ellis's eyes.

"Does he look innocent?" Buttkiss said, and stared gravely at Brown.

Brown looked at Robinson and noticed his head had dropped and hung to his neck as if strung by a piece of thread.

Brown's gaze jumped from the kid in the car to Ellis and then to Buttkiss, who was looking suspiciously at Brown.

"Henry," he said, and shined the light at him.

The light was blindingly bright, and Brown had to squint. He wondered how Mort Ellis had kept his eyes wide the whole time.

He must be high, Brown decided.

"Yes, Karl, I'm on it."

Brown walked to the back of the car and grabbed the latch of the trunk. Fear struck him and his body numbed. He gulped down the fear and bit his lips.

The latch clicked and he lifted the lid.

He pulled it up all the way and gazed inside to find it empty.

Relief shot through him, and he sighed.

"What is it?" Buttkiss shouted.

"It's empty."

"Okay, Mort," he said to the kid. "You're good to go."

Ellis looked at Brown and then at his friend in the back, nodded, then turned to hop in the front.

"You okay?" Buttkiss asked as Ellis drove away.

"Yeah, I'm fine," Brown said, and the two of them exchanged glanced.

They walked over to the cruiser, parked out of the way, and opened the doors and stepped inside.

"Okay," Buttkiss said, and revved the engine.

As Buttkiss turned the wheel slightly to the left and the cruiser rolled out of the breakdown lane, a voice came through the radio saying, "A blue Subaru spotted on Lake Drive. Might be our guy."

"Let's get this asshole," Buttkiss said, ramming the gas pedal into the floor.

Runaway

The sun sets as I walk home from school. Darkness overtakes everything I know. I get to the end of my street, see my house—my parents' house glowing bright against the stark buildings to its left and right. I start down the street, and as I come closer to my house, my home, the light fades, starts blackening, darkening, the only light left exploding from the window of my parents' bedroom. Only the light up there isn't the least bit inviting. It's a dark crimson, like spilt blood, and the milling silhouettes that dance on the glass—they look like witches, like warlocks, brooding mutants brewing their perverse, poisonous magic.

The black creatures, illuminated by a single glowing bulb, morph and mutate on the windowpane, vividly twisted, black slashes cutting the glass like the eyes of cats. Standing there, staring up at the sick images, I turn and run, back up the street, cut left and lose myself in the nihilistic meadows—the park immersed in darkness.

I can only see a few feet in front of me, can only smell a vague sour scent that wasps up my nostrils, can only hear the flicking of a lighter, the bickering of two subhumans huddled in the darkness, highlighted by a flickering bulb that swings above them, and behind them looms a wall painted with names and terrifying tags. The two lost boys divert their eyes from the pipe and lock me in their sights—they follow my tread with their mutant eyes. I can sense their heads turning as I walk, can feel their beady eyes burning inside their skulls, the fires licking and thrashing at their brains, the smell of burning bones whisked away on the wind, carried up my nose, and I cringe.

And then the sound of their shoes slapping the cold concrete, coming toward me, slivers down my spine and makes me shiver. I pick up my pace, falling into a fierce and pointed stride. I hear a hushed voice, sharp and curt in its aloneness, the sound of one of them muttering—

"Let's get him."

I feel their breath brushing against my bare skin, the stunning scent coming from their mouths. The hand grasping my shoulder. I whirl around, spinning free of his attempt to grab me, and hurry away, through the dark depths of nothingness, going nowhere fast, through the blackness, the wind stabbing me like a switchblade, like a straight-razor, the cutting cold whipping me, lapping at my wounds, stabbing and thrashing, *brrrr!!!*

The sound of their shoes pounding the pavement, replaced with a muffled thudding, sneakers beating the cold, wet grass—it dies away, and I'm left alone with my own thoughts, birds squawking in the trees, red eyes peering out from black slits in the stillness.

Bats!!!

Runaway

Their squawking grows, as though they're talking about me—up on their perches, in the safety of the trees, hidden behind leaves and branches. Peering at me. They gawk, and they squawk, and there's a sudden rustle of tree branches, bats scattering into the sky, wings flapping, bats hissing, screeching, scurrying like rats—so sudden that I stop for a beat. I stop and listen, stop and wait, listening to the hissing, and then I walk on.

As I head to the exit of the park, I lift my hood and pull it up over my head. The hood caves in around my face. I keep a steady pace, not to disturb the chaos above me, the bats gathering, swarming the sky like fighter pilots, dive-bombing.

Then, I hear a series of chirps, a round of fierce and frightening sounds that causes my nerves to churn. For the first time I know they've spotted me, because up in the sky these bats are coming together to form a dark and eerie wall, with bricks rippling and flittering; then another chirp, and they charge me like bullets, nip me like puppies, their sharp beaks pinching and pulling, slashing my skin with quick jabs, ripping off bits of flesh and flying away.

Pain shoots through my veins, as cold as ice and blistering hot like flickering flames. A crucial ache claws at my bones, strains my muscles and leverages my joints the wrong way. White-hot and sharp, it feels as if my eyes are bleeding, leaking brain fluids.

My feet speed up, my knees bouncing, my pace quickening to a dash, my hands slapping away their vicious attacks. I'm running now, through the dark wall of flying, fluttering rats, wings flapping and slapping. They nip and they tug, ripping me apart bit by bit, with quick dives and evasive measures. They're fast, these bats—swooping down from the sky, shooting toward me like heat-seeking

57

missiles, their beaks pinching and pulling flesh. They're so quick they look like flashes. They look like arrows fired from crossbows.

I finally make it through the wall of bats and reach the street, a car speeding past in a flash, so fast my head nearly spins off. My neck cranes and my eyes follow the next passing vehicle—a van shooting past in a blur of bright red light. It crosses my path, and then, as I move to cross the street, a horn honks at me and an unidentified sports car flies by, giving me a kick in the ass for not looking both ways.

On my second attempt at crossing, this time scanning the street with frightened eyes, I spot, in the not-too-far off distance, a gruff-looking old man lumbering down the side of the street, a sign hanging over his front and his back, held together with strings wrapped over his shoulders. Straining my sight, I see what the sign says—

On the front: "Ninjas killed my parents. Need money for Kung Fu lessons." And on the back: "But I'll probably just get drunk instead. Please help this desperate old fool get wasted so he doesn't have to live through another night homeless and sober."

I instantly feel bad for the "old fool," a guilty feeling twisting my gut, squeezing it so tight I feel like vomiting.

"Hey," I shout across the street, waving my hands above me.

He turns and looks at me, stopping dead-still on the side of the street.

"Over here."

He starts toward me, stepping down from the curb, and nearly tumbling when a corvette comes crashing out of nowhere and nearly collides with his drunken self. He steps back on the curb, twists his ankle, and plops on his butt.

I hurry over, checking if he's okay.

Runaway

I reach the other side and stick out my right hand to help him up. He grabs my hand with a grimy glove and uses my leverage to hoist himself up. Then I hear a click. A sharp, unsettling noise that sounds so suddenly my heart stops cold, my skin crawling. My blood stills, my heart jumps, and I see the switchblade in his left hand. He holds it out, and its yellowish surface gleams, juxtaposed against the black encompassing the blade. I take a step back as he thrusts it at me.

As it comes closer I suck in my gut, the blade slicing through nothing but air, doing a full circle, before he regains control of the dicing knife. I don't know what to do—on the one hand there's the street with its fast-moving cars, which are just waiting to crash into me and take me out for good (I know they are); and on the other hand there's this man standing before me, waiting to slice me open, to steal the cash I don't have, and to feed on my dead flesh—*the cash I don't have!*

It comes to me like a sucker punch, powerful and unexpected, and I hold out my hands in surrender. "No, wait, stop! I don't have any money."

He steps forward and presses the cold blade to my throat. With one hand holding it firm and secure against my neck, the raw power of its cutting edge biting down hard on my flesh, he pats me down with his other hand. He goes over the already checked spots a second time, and then again. The blade then retreats in on itself, locking in place inside the handle.

He turns and walks away.

Jeremy Void

A Bag Full of God

Andy, what a meathead, said he could cook the cocaine into crack. No problem. He said he could, but he
cooked the crap out of it and now we're left with this
miniscule bag of powder and Andy gets none. Sara, she's screaming her face off at Andy, calling him shit-for-brains. David, he's
pacing the room, talking to himself, like he's the only one here.
He's really worried. What're we gonna do? I hear him say over
and over again.

Kristina is saying the same, though not to herself, but to me,
sitting on the couch beside me, pestering me and yelling and saying
why don't I fuckin listen to her. I hear her, I do, but I don't care.

I stand up and reach in my pocket and pull out my cellphone
and make a call. I can barely hear the ringing over the ruckus
Sara's making. I look over at her and shush her with my finger.

Don't you shush me! she yells and storms around the counter
and out of the kitchen and waves a bony finger at my face.

I grab her finger and twist it in my hand, and she cringes just as someone says, Hello?

Tony, I say into the phone, holding tight to Sara's finger. A forty bag.

He says okay, and Sara and I are now in the truck riding to Tony's place.

My teeth grind. Crackling.

Sara doesn't speak. The radio plays quietly, and I think it's the Circle Jerks.

We're almost there, she's thinking. Yay, we're almost there. She looks at me and smiles and it looks grotesque the color of her teeth, so green and gross and capped with mold and scum. She looks away and jerks the wheel to the side and the truck dodges a parked car and we glide up an incline and slow to a shuddering stop in three parking spots in the lot outside of Tony's place.

She honks the horn, and my stomach churns with the annoying sound.

She honks it again, and I can tell she's not too happy with the noise, either, but still she honks one more time and the door opens up and a beam of light shines through and crafts a fabulous glowing rectangle that stands out against the darkness and in the bright doorway a dark figure materializes, just a silhouette, and starts down the steps. He has a skip in his step, and a glide to his stride, and his face comes into focus, it's Tony's face, and his knuckles come down on the driver's side window, with a clunk-clunk-clunk.

Sara rolls down her window, passes him the cash, and he chucks a bag of fine, white powder in through the window and it lands on my lap. I hold it up and the light from the door makes the bag sparkle and little glittery beads flicker and I feel like I'm holding a bag full of God Himself.

As Tony walks away, Sara stomps on the gas and the truck tears out of the lot in a surge of glory. The excitement makes me horny.

Sara looks at me and smiles again, and this time I see past the horrific grin and she looks so beautiful now, my stunningly hot girl-friend.

I stare out the window and watch the apartment buildings shoot past in a yellowish red blur of light, and watch through the front windshield the traffic lights changing from green to orange to red and then cast a green glow on the windshield as we float beneath.

I can't wait, I say to Sara, who turns the wheel smoothly to the left, and the truck bounces and lands softly and we go up and over a small hill and then stop.

My gaze circles the lot in which we've stopped, and in front of the truck is the back wall of a McDonald's, just a wall made of bricks with a dumpster to the right. I watch customers appear from the side and enter their cars and drive away. Their head- and taillights carve smudged lines in the night.

I then hear a shrill tapping, and my eyes find the source: a mirror laid flat in between our seats, with cocaine piled in the center and a razor blade slicing through the chunks and softening the powder. My heart picks up its pace when I see this. It starts jackhammering in my chest, and in my arms and legs I feel the force of my blood pumping and flowing faster, my pulse pounding harder, the blood speeding through my veins with sharp perseverance. Sara cuts the coke with perfect adherence. She looks like a pro as she slides her ATM card along the mirror and carves out four tasty lines. I touch the tip of my tongue to the tip of my pointer and press my pointer finger to the end of a line, really rub it in, but only the end, coating my finger with that delicious white powder. I rub it along my gum and my gum starts to feel tingly and soon goes numb and I smile watching Sara do the same, slathering her gum with cocaine.

I crane my neck and look out the rear window, and into an empty spot across the lot rolls a police cruiser and its headlights bounce off the fence and then shut off. Darkness eats the cruiser and I can only see a silhouette of the cop exit the car and he starts straight for us.

5-O! I shout.

What? Sara cranes her neck and says, Shit.

She slams her hand on the mirror's edge and the flat piece of glass jumps and flips over and the cocaine scatters like dust.

I look over there, and the cop's almost here, so Sara dumps the bag out of her slightly open window and rolls it all the way up and wraps her arms around me and rams her lips into mine and stuffs her tongue inside my mouth. It feels its way down my throat and swirls and weaves and wrestles with my own tongue, dancing with it now, and it feels so good the way it swirls around and caresses my tongue.

My dick fills with blood, and I feel it hardening in my pants as she moves her hands up and down my back, and then come the clunks and she stops and turns and the cop is out there staring at us.

The window eases down inch by inch and the cop looks in very sternly at us, and when I maneuver my gaze back to the rear window I spot another cop on his way over, and the one who stands outside the window has a nametag with the insignia KANE. He crouches down and then rises and his stern features sharpen.

What's this? he says, and brings a small plastic bag into view.

Uh…. Sara fumbles with her words, unsure of what to say or if she should even say anything at all, so I chime in with, That's not ours.

The cop shakes his head and the second cop joins him and Kane says, Get out of the truck.

Sir, it's not ours, I repeat, regretting that we'd wasted the blow, for the second time tonight, because if he lets us go, we're out of dough and can't exactly get more, not until the morning. Really, sir, we've just come to make out.

Get out, the second cop says, smiling.

Something about his snide smile doesn't sit right in my gut, but still I do as I'm told and the cops shove the both of us against the side of the truck, read us our rights, bind us in cuffs, and shove us away toward the cruiser and push down on our heads as we duck under the roof and settle in the backseat. Sara sits to the left of me.

The cruiser rolls backwards and does a one-point maneuver that brings the front end forward and then we all are off, out of the lot, and in the front the two cops talk and laugh and joke and laugh and the numbness in my gums fades and becomes itchy and I scratch it with my tongue as stores whiz by and the sirens come on and we soar under a traffic light, with an array of red and blue lights flashing all around, and then the sirens go off but the cruiser keeps forward and the cops in the front talk and laugh and joke and laugh and their voices irritate me in a way I can't articulate, just a nuisance of noise that nags at my brain and my eardrums thunder in pain.

My teeth grind. Crackling.

I watch the gas station attendant feed gas into a blue Subaru and then see the lights in a Starbucks shut off all of a sudden and watch a hooker stand on the corner and she walks down a side street when she obviously sees us and the cops I can tell saw her too because in the front they crack jokes about this derelict woman, and about what she is, and this makes me mad as she probably needs the cash, maybe to feed her two crying babies she's got at home, but then she shouldn't have had the babies in the first place but at the same time I feel guilty for thinking so negatively about her and I wonder what her name is and I know I'll never know and then the cruiser stops.

I shift my gaze nervously and to our sides, out the windows, are boarded-up buildings, and through the front windshield I see a dead end, blocked off by a short fence and beyond it are woods and what the fuck!

This can't be good.

I, for the first time this whole ride, look at Sara and her jaw is moving, I know this from the way her bone pokes through her cheek and then her cheek deflates and she does it again, and I look in the front, but … where'd they go?

I hear a click which steals my focus to the door and it opens on my side and on Sara's side and the second cop is standing right outside, still smiling like a madman.

I look over at Sara and past her is Kane and he says to her, Get out.

A Bag Full of God

Sara's jaw moves faster and I hear the sound of her teeth grinding, or maybe that's mine, I don't know.

Get out, the second cop says to me, and, unlike Sara, I obey right away, nervously though, and over my shoulder Kane drags her out by her hair and then she's gone.

My line of sight bypasses the roof and I don't even see her across the cruiser, and that's when it comes—the *BANG!*, my head clanging into the steal fender, and then the *WHOMP!*, my neck snapping and my head smacking the concrete, a *CRUNCH!*, a boot barreling into my ribs, and I fold, try to fend off the next shot with my hands, but in my ring finger I feel a stabbing throb when the boot cuts through and connects with my gut.

Tears roll down my face and feel like ice.

The cop reaches down, lifts me up, shoves me against the cruiser, and drives his bony knee into my stomach, and I fold and he throws me down and my body dives headlong and the top of my dome whacks the ground and my lights go out.

When my lights come back on, my sight wavering, with blurry lines of static jumping and weaving and fading in and out of focus, the world turning upside-down and coming back around and flattening—when I come to and the world stops moving, I realize I'm sitting up against the cruiser, my butt on the ground, blood distorting my vision so everything is tainted with a crimson shade, and I feel a thin line of fluid drip past my nose, and the two cops, I see now, are smoking cigarettes and talking in muffled voices I can't make out.

I look around for Sara but don't see her anywhere. They could have killed her, I wonder, but then she comes into view when I peer underneath the cruiser, and she looks dead, lying dull on the ground, and I have to do something now.

The cops aren't paying much attention to me, maybe they assume I'm out for the count, but they're wrong because I surge up to my feet and tear the gun from Kane's holster with amazing speed and agility and this heroic act grabs their attention and directs it toward me.

Don't move! I shout, clumsily holding and waving the gun in both hands, and they take a step back and then another and a third.

I said don't move!

The second cop reaches for his holster and I take aim and fire and try to hit him in the leg, but instead the bullet hits the ground and dings and bounces and goes somewhere else. I look that way, then through my peripheral vision I see him reach for his gun again and I take aim again and hold the pistol firm.

Their hands drift up cautiously.

We can talk this through, says Kane.

I shake my head no.

Put the gun down, the second cop says, demonstrating what he means by pushing down with his hands, as though pushing down the trunk of a car.

I step forward and stab the air with the gun. Keep your hands up!

We can work something out.

Just put it down.

It's okay, you'll see, just put it down and we'll figure this out.

No, I bark. Gimme the keys!

A Bag Full of God

Kane reaches for the set dangling from his belt loop and I get nervous and fire at his leg again but miss again and the bullet sails off into the distance.

His hands fly up fast.

Now the keys, I say. Toss em to me.

I wave my fingers in a beckoning motion, indicating to hand them over, and I hear a grunt and turn and the cops advance and I turn and they step back.

I said don't move!

Kane flings me the keys and I reach out to catch them but they bounce off my hand and I accidentally squeeze off another shot, this one high, and when I look up, blood is squirting out of where the second cop's ear should be. Fuck me! I pick up the keys and jump in the cruiser, behind the wheel, and the cruiser goes forward and almost crashes into the fence ... but I catch it before it connects, shift into reverse, ride the gas as the cruiser backs out, shift into drive, floor it, and the cruiser roars as I sail away.

But I forgot Sara.

I look out the rearview mirror and lights appear everywhere, red and blue splashes sprinkling the darkness, and I realize I can't turn back now.

I speed down a few blocks and take a few turns and end up back where it all started, outside Kristina's apartment, where Andy fucked up big, and the lights are still on and I wonder what they're doing up there.

As I climb the tall stairway to Kristina's pad on the second to last floor and as my lungs start to burn and my heavy breathing gets raspier with each step and each floor I pass, the smell of crack, which is sweet like black licorice but tinted with something bitter, grows inside my nose, and I know exactly what they're doing, and when I open the door I see Kristina lying on the floor and Andy lying on the couch and gray, transparent rings rising from Kristina's mouth as Andy holds a metal one-hitter to his lips and holds a lighter in front of the small bowl and he roasts the rock inside and envy comes at me like a five-ton bus and knocks me back a few feet, when I notice they're missing their TV.

At that I smile.

When I go over to them and sit down on the floor with my back to the couch, sighing with great relief, Kristina rolls onto her stomach and a pipe drops from above to in front of me, and I take that as my cue to hold the flame a little bit away from the rock and it sizzles and melts as I pull the toxic smoke in and down my throat and I hold the smoke in as long as I can and, when I can't take the pressure building up in my lungs any longer, let go of the smoke and it pours out like water gushing through a hole in a dam—an overload of pleasure, a release of pressure, my eyes widening, my lips drying, my body rising—and I'm flying now, hovering above the couch and holding out my hand, where the pipe sits on my palm undisturbed.

Seconds go by, and then maybe a whole minute before Andy lifts the pipe from my palm and drops it saying, Fuck, it's hot.

It is? I say, dumbfounded.

Kristina rolls onto her back and kicks her legs in a spasm of insane laughter.

Suddenly the door swings open and smacks the wall with an earsplitting crack that grabs my focus, Sara standing in its wake, and I remember then that I left her back there and I kinda care but think of it as only a minor mishap and she's filthy, dirt-ridden, with thick red goo matting her hair, and blood flowing from her nose, and a swollen bottom lip, and a black ring circling her right eye.

She limps over to us, sits down beside me, and says, You won't believe what happened.

Kristina stops laughing and looks gravely at her friend.

Andy exhales a stream of vapor and hands Sara the pipe and she takes a hit, sitting there beside me, and then she proceeds:

Well, you see. The cops picked up me and him—pointing at me—and brought us to a backstreet, and this one cop named Kane pulled me outta the cruiser and booted me in the face. Everything after that point seems unclear till I heard the roar of tires grinding the ground and I angled my head and saw the cruiser pull away.

We were safe, I thought. I thought we were safe. I called out his name—gesturing at me again, with her head—but he didn't respond. It kinda reminded me of the time when I'd got picked up for disorderly conduct outside the shopping mall and I called you—referring to me—and you never came to pay my bail, cuz you were drunk and didn't feel like it was a good idea to drive drunk to a police station and walk inside, remember that?

I nod at her.

You're such a fuckin asshole, y'know that?

I smirk and a chuckle slips out.

I spent my entire fuckin weekend there all cuz you had to save your face. You fuckin prick!

Her hand flies back and comes crashing forward and I move my head out from its warpath, and it sails by in a flash.

Chill out! Kristina says.

Yeah, calm down, says Andy, passing her the pipe.

She takes a good-sized hit and gives the pipe to Andy, who replenishes the bowl with another rock.

So what happened next? Andy says.

What do you mean? She says it so seriously, not a hint of humor on her screwed-up face.

You came to, Kristina reminds her. You know, after the cop kicked you in the head?

Oh yeah … wait, no … no, yeah yeah … no, wait, hold on a sec. I needa think. The room's spinning and I can't focus with all this fuckin noise. Everybody shut up for a sec and lemme fuckin think!

We all stare at her quietly—expectantly.

Okay, she starts up again. So I came to and I heard screaming going on—the crack sizzling as Kristina takes a hit—and when I looked to the side I saw the one cop swatting at his ear as though swatting at a swarm of flies, and the other one was calling for backup. They didn't much care for me.

She stops talking and Andy takes the pipe and pulls and passes it to me and I pass it to Sara and she passes it to Kristina and it's not until Andy takes it back that she proceeds with the story:

So I pushed myself up and kinda stumbled away and when I got to the street I stuck out my thumb and the first car to come pulled to a stop at my feet, and I got in.

It was a college kid kinda guy and he expected me to do him favors, which I wouldn't do, and so he told me to get out of the car, but instead I slapped him hard in the face and shoved him out while the car kept going and I stayed in and slid behind the wheel and all round me there were flashing red and blue lights. I thought maybe there was a fire going on somewhere. I turned the car and went in the way of the lights, and soaring past in the opposite lane was a line of cop cruisers, so I did another U-turn, cutting across the median, cuz I had a burning desire to see that fire, and then I.... She coughs, and the raspy sound comes out all nasty.

It's then when, suddenly, the shame for leaving her behind starts racking my brain, and I can feel beads of sweat starting to bubble on my face. I wipe away the sweat on my forehead with my shirtsleeve, and look to Andy, whose worried expression tells me we're out of crack, and the fact that his teeth grind gives me the frights, and Sara, she's still telling the story, but Kristina, I can tell, is not paying any attention, anxiety plastered to her face, and the story Sara's telling starts to waver, starts to make no sense, the little events seeming more humdrum with each minute.

Sara's head weaves, searching for something, as I stand up and start scanning the floor. Maybe someone dropped a piece. It's possible, it's happened before. Andy is rummaging through the couch and Kristina is counting her cash—she counts it again and again, double-checking her math. The walls are closing in around me, and I don't know what to do, I don't know what to do, I don't know what to do.

Panic, *panic—PANIC!*

I reach in my pocket and pull out my cellphone and make a call. The crude ringing sounds like a razor lodged in my brain.

Hello?

Tony, I say into the phone, the commotion quieting, all eyes on me....

Jeremy Void

Nefarious Endeavor #2

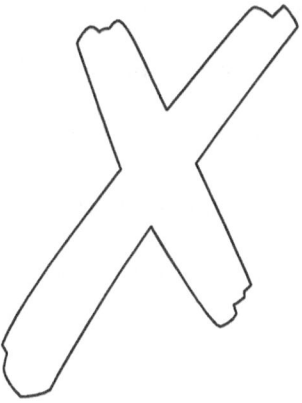

There were three loud knocks.

Melrose stirred in his bed, rolled onto his side, onto his stomach. Three more knocks. He sat up and rubbed the sleep from his eyes. Who could it be at this time? He looked at the clock and saw it was two a.m. Saw it was the middle of the night. He wanted to stay asleep. He wanted to sleep until the morning, until the alarm clock woke him at seven sharp. But now it was two a.m. Startled from sleep, he said, "Who is it?"

"Room service," said the voice on the other side of the door.

"It's two a.m."

"Room service," the voice said again.

Melrose grunted. He stood up in only his boxers and a white T-shirt. The covers where he'd slept were all ruffled. He went to the dresser and looked at the mirror hanging on the side. He had grown a five-o'clock shadow in the night. He hated dealing with people when he was unshaven. He looked at the clock again, and the blinking numbers read two-o'two. He grunted. Coughed. He went back to the bed.

Three knocks again.

"Coming," he said.

He grabbed the pack of cigarettes set on his nightstand and removed a smoke and lit it up and took in a long haul. It relieved him immediately. He felt relaxed and went to the door. In only his boxers. He stopped with his hand on the knob. Looked down. He was only in his boxers. He turned around and went back to the dresser.

There was another round of knocks.

He opened the top drawer and pulled out a pair of sweatpants. He flapped them in the air and pulled them open at the waistband and stepped inside. He pulled them up his legs and turned toward the door.

Three more knocks.

"What is it?" he said as he twisted the knob and pulled the door open.

A chirp from a silenced handgun and the bullet sliced through his head.

My First Date

A True Account

I've been with many girls, but on only one date. So I was nervous. The plan was to take her to dinner (Panera Bread) on the gift card I stole from a customer while working there. The customer passed me the card, I slid it through the reader and slipped it into my pocket, and passed back a blank one—real smooth. Then after dinner I would take her to the Music Gym, a small section of this warehouse where bands paid the two hapless goons who worked there five dollars to practice in one of the three rooms inside, and my band practiced there at least once a week. I was to take her to my band practice, impress her, then take her home—that was my plan, but who would have known I'd just end up at the bar drinking by myself before practice started?

I sure as hell didn't. I should have, but I didn't.

Once, I was on the train, and across from me was this young girl with big breasts wearing a striped shirt who kept looking at me like there was something on my face or a booger hanging out my nose or something caught in my teeth. I looked back, and in her eyes I could tell there was something shy about her. She had this baby face that was really cute, and her overall image, her clothes, still a bit fashionable for my taste, looked so neat on her, as if she were going for something in style mixed with a hint of rebellion. She looked like an innocent little girl seeking danger, which is probably the reason for what happened next.

The train careened around the corner and then slowed and stopped. She got up and started for the door. On her way she stopped to my right and slipped me a folded piece of white paper. It was strange. Once she handed me that paper, I was stunned. I went into a daze. My eyes followed her out the train and I watched her disappear as the train sped off. When she was fully gone from my sight I turned my focus to that folded piece of white paper, and opened it. Written inside the fold was I THINK YOU'RE CUTE. Beneath the inscription was a dash, followed by her name and number. I waited a few days before I called her.

When I finally did, she set up times where we would meet on the phone and see if we were compatible for each other. I went along only because I was bored and I had nothing better to do. Our first phone date went like this:

What do you like to do for fun? she said.

Drink, I said.

Do you like to do anything else?

Uh, music. I like music, too.

I don't think we're right for each other. *Click.*

So it went like that. And now I was at home, psyched for my first ever date. I was jittery too. What if things went wrong? Shit. Before I knew it my head was hovering over a couple lines of Adderal, and I blasted them up my nose, straightened myself, looked

My First Date

in the mirror, flirted with my image for a minute, then stomped down the stairs and left.

I remember I was so wired my teeth were grinding something fierce, making abrasive crunching and cracking sounds, and when I got off at Kenmore and waited for the next train to come, I chatted with these two high school girls there, who mostly kept their mouths shut while I did all the talking, and boy, did I talk; I wouldn't stop, not for anything, not even a single breath between words, whereas all they could hear was probably the rickety-rack of my teeth. I should have been ashamed of myself, but the speed took care of that.

I told them about how I was on my way to my first date, I told them about how I was quite nervous, I told them that to take care of my worrisome nerves I blew some Adderal, and is it noticeable, I mean am I noticeably high, seriously do you think she'd be able to tell? I asked in a frantic panic.

They shook their heads and said, No, you'll be fine. Or at least that's what I remember them saying, and we all know memories don't mean a thing. I hopped on the next train and sat in the back. I watched Boston University speed past me. Right after Boston University, I got off.

It wasn't long before I saw her. I recognized her face from the picture she'd posted online, though I was mildly disappointed, because from the looks of it she seemed a few pounds overweight. But I was already there, and there was no turning back now.

When I was about sixteen I went out with this one girl whose name will remain a mystery. This girl found me on AOL Instant Messenger. She said we were in the hospital together—NEVER GO OUT WITH A GIRL YOU MET IN THE HOSPITAL!

She told me her name, and I didn't recall it, so she told me the names of some other kids who were in the hospital the same time as us. I recognized their names right away, and for a moment I thought this girl I was messaging was that one girl I hooked up with a few times in the hospital. We made a date to meet, and I guess you could call this date a "date." It was, in a way.

Since I had no car and she lived all the way out in Quincy, Mass., I phoned my good friend Andy and asked him to chauffer. I asked him to come along—for we were only going to see a movie and it wouldn't take long. I was so excited, because this beautiful girl I met in the hospital had found me online and I was on my way to meet her, Andy behind the wheel.

But I was wrong, of course. It wasn't her. The girl coming out the door seemed to have down-syndrome or something. Her lop-sided, pockmarked face and big nose didn't look good on her; it wasn't a good look. Trust me, I know. But being that I was a decent young man—for this had all happened before I flipped, because if it had happened after the fact, I would have told Andy to stomp the gas and his car would have lurched forward and fled the scene as if we'd just robbed a bank—I decided to give her an honest chance. We went and saw a movie, and that turned into the worst six months of my teenage life.

But now, twenty-one-years old, I stood on one side of the train tracks and I watched this gleeful young girl about my age cutting across and I said hi and we walked away. She was really sweet, and I kind of feel bad, but on the other hand, I suppose I taught her a valuable lesson about meeting guys online—because for all I know the next guy could have been a rapist. Come to think of it, I probably saved that young girl's life. I should be proud of myself.

My First Date

I did a good deed that day. All we did was walk about a mile down Commonwealth Avenue before she turned to me and said she had a lot of homework to do and she better get going. I said bye, she didn't.

I took a right and instead found myself seated all alone at O'Brien's Pub, sipping on a Guinness in the dark.

Black-and-Blue

The Art of Fucking Up

The line of urine sprays from my cock, arcing and splashing on the window of Domino's Pizza, the big front window that looks into the whole forefront of the store. The woman at the counter stares and blushes, taking an order, I assume, on the phone, while her eyes point downward and try to avoid marveling at the massive prick pumping piss into the window. She likes it, and the stream keeps on coming. Then it dwindles, trickling at my feet, and finally stops.

I tuck my dick back inside my pants and kinda shuffle as I pull them up my waist, zip the fly, and button up. Behind me Craig is hollering, telling me to hurry up and get back inside the car. The cocaine is waiting for me.

"It's being patient," he says, "very patient, but you and I both know patience is a vice and the coke will find this out itself given time." And he laughs, the sound gargled and goofy, drunk in its own right.

I turn around and see Craig sitting in the front seat leering out the window and laughing and glaring at my legs. I follow his glare, and—fuck me—my jeans are darkening. I realize then that I haven't stopped pissing.

But fuck it! It's only piss. I got coke to look forward to.

I go around the front of his car, clapping my hand on the hood with hard deliverance to let him know I'm coming. When I reach the passenger side, he leans over and unlatches the door, as it won't open from the outside, and I slide inside. Next to the seat, a CD case is laid on the armrest, or whatever you would call that thing that opens and closes for the sake of stashing one's drugs. Two lines of cocaine—looking so incredibly appetizing that my mouth waters with delight and I have to lick the spittle from my lips to keep from drooling—are prepared for the taking.

My buddy Craig, he rolls a one-dollar bill and weasels it up his nose, lowers his head and then pulls up through the tube one of the lines. I watch his eyes grow as an automatic result, my own eyes shifting from his to the CD case and then back to his brown glazed and dilated dots. I'm so looking forward to that initial thrill, the hard punch ramming into my heart, and the taste that comes moments later, when my throat starts numbing and maybe burns a bit, but that's the best part, when the hit really kicks in.

He raises his head and with a smile slips me the dollar bill, and I do the same, taking the whole line like a pro.

It comes crashing up my nostril, the sensation a mix between abrasive and soft, tearing and soothing, and delivering a blow of epic proportion. The force like having a horse drive its hind hooves into my chest. Not an unpleasant feeling.

Black-and-Blue

I finish devouring the line and oh how relieved I feel, as though having woken up on my own accord after a night of sleeping as soundly as a drugged-up hound, my skin warm with delight as the car opens up and allows more room to breathe. It's magnificent, and Craig, when I assume he catches the hint of a smile on my face, shifts the car into reverse, backs up a bit, and guns it out of the lot as I fiddle with the radio dial—a talk show announcer jabbering mindlessly about unimportant current events, a fizz of feedback, some lame pop song, another talk show, some more static, the news, the weather, and I insert my own CD.

We drive along for a little while, taking lefts and rights, until we enter and descend the onramp of the highway. The car speeds up and edges sideways and continues that way till we merge into the farthest left lane, and then the car kicks it forward, a jerk and a jolting pull thrusting us along with the sudden change of speed.

And remember that taste I was talking about? Well, it hits me right now, and the car, I notice, is flying off the ground, faster than I've ever seen a car go. It soars like a rocket ship, hitting ruts and bumps, bouncing on its shocks. The music I've chosen to play is fast and hard-hitting, heavy like a brick, smashing around the insides of my ears, a smile eating my face. I slip my sunglasses on and look in the mirror, and a rockstar stares back at me, so stunningly handsome. My head bounces on my neck, and I even hold up my right hand like the sign of the devil as I bob and glower. I'm an unstoppable force, flying down the highway in the fastest lane, sitting beside Craig, whose eyes are centered on the road, focused like a dog protecting its bone. The music makes the mood of the moment seem more real, more vivacious and romantic, a gigantic

93

relaxed feeling I suddenly want more of. We glide along, my head nodding up and down, the bounces resembling a rollercoaster ride.

I'm so full of glee right now, so full of wonder and excitement, that I never want to come down.

When I glance out my own window the other cars on the road seem to be soaring by even faster. That's weird.

I turn the volume down and say to Craig, *How fast are we going?*—suddenly aware that my mind might be playing a trick.

He cranes his head and says, *Eighty, why? Turn the music back up.*
Don't you hear the other cars honking?
Yeah, probably some hot chick hitchhiking.
Seriously, Craig, how fast?
Seriously, Dave, I don't fuckin care or know. Fast!
Look at the speedometer, you fuckin ass.

He angles his head and his smile shifts into surprise. *Fuck, we're only going forty.* And his smile comes back, the two of us laughing loud and out of control, the car wavering to and fro.

Cars are honking at us, I tell him.

I know. At that his laughter only grows, but then falters when flashing red and blue lights brighten the highway, reflecting off the rearview mirror. And his laughter immediately ceases, as does mine.

He slows the car and drifts as far right as he can to the side.

My nerves explode with fear. My heart starts beating mega fast.

I crane my head frantically. My eyes scan the street.

The flow of cars is slowing until there are none on the road anymore, all of them having drifted to the side.

I hate my life, is what I'm thinking as the cruiser pulls behind us and the sirens shut off.

My stomach clenches and sweat streams down my face, my hands wet and anxious.

Time all of a sudden slows. Everything gets quiet and sounds distant. A loud pounding in my ears, rhythmic. The door of the cruiser cranes outward and a boot materializes.

It touches the ground and a second boot follows.

What the fuck! I utter, but I don't think Craig can hear.

His face is frozen forward and his eyes are focused on the road ahead. I don't know how he can be so still at a time like this. This is not good, not one bit.

The cop is coming toward the car, one step after another.

And then time resumes its normal speed, and the cop is saying, "Do you know how fast you were going?"

Craig doesn't speak. I lean over and whisper in his ear, *Don't tell him. It's all a test.*

"Do you know how fast you were going?"

Craig's head starts its cycle, and eventually he is returning eye contact with the cop.

He says, *Uh ... what?*

"How fast were you going?"

Craig's head rotates again until he is facing me, and I shake my head. Don't say anything, I want to tell him. Don't you dare speak!

"Can you please step out of the car, sir?"

He slowly obeys, and that's when I notice his skin is quivering.

Jeremy Void

Fuck this.......................

....

    I'm out of the car, slamming the door hard and bolting down the side of the highway. I'm almost caught up to the cruiser and behind it, when the door clicks open and a black man tackles me to the ground.

He throws cuffs around my wrists as I struggle to break free.

I scream and wriggle on the ground now. His knee grinds my backbone.

Let me fuckin go! I shout, almost crying.

I whip my head back, aimed to smash him in the chin, but he catches my hair in his hand and slams my face into the street, now held down on my cheek.

Seriously, man, I holler at him like a deranged freak. *Seriously, do you know who the* fuck *I am?* Spit sprays from my mouth as I continue shouting.

"No," he says sternly, holding my head firm on the ground. "I don't *know* who the fuck you are." I feel his breath on the back of my neck. "Shut up," he commands, keeping himself calm. "Hey, you think we should call an ambulance?"

In the distance: "Probably."

He holds me there for a long time. I watch them direct Craig past my head, his feet coming real close, and lead him into the backseat of the cruiser.

The other cop—the one not holding me down, his boots only inches from my face—says real calm-like, "You have the right to remain silent—"

Black-and-Blue

Fuck you! I snap, and laugh slightly, like it's all a joke. *I said fuck you.*

The cop pulls up on my hair, my head going with it, and drives me back down, the feeling of the crash like fire ants chomping on my skin. It burns. My eyes water.

Fuck you, I spit one last time, feeling winded, deflated. Defeated. It's no use fighting them. They'll only win.

Jeremy Void

Single-Mindlessness

The wolf howled at the full moon. The howl droned and
rose again. Three yips, and a droning sound. Thin wisps
of clouds drifted in front of the golden circle. It gave off an
eerie effect, an effect perfect for tonight, for the townsfolk came in
a cluster, hooting and hollering. The horses' hooves thudded and
the torches flickered. Pitchforks loomed over the mob. They
clawed at the sky, as the wolf's cry dwindled. Then it was silent.
All the sounds now arose from the townsfolk. Shouting, anger and
distaste mixed in with the hate.

Leading the mob was Nathaniel Helms, who held a pitchfork in
his left hand and a flickering torch in his right. Beside him was his
brother, Bartholomew, who rode his horse and wielded a six-
shooter, with a shotgun lain across the saddle. Their mother,
Marge, and their father, Ralph, walked a couple steps behind.
And behind them was an angry mob. The Helms family had orga-
nized the attack. Had gathered the townsfolk and rounded the

horses. Had supplied the pitchforks and torches. Had told them all to go home and get their guns. Meet us here in an hour.

And they all had.

Presently the house in question was getting closer. It was a big mansion, dark and dreary.

Nathaniel stopped and Bartholomew's horse halted. Marge and Ralph stopped too, as did the mob.

"We're almost there!" Nathaniel shouted.

Chanting and cheering and ranting and raving, the tips of torches banging the ground, the tips of pitchforks thudding and thumping, voices hooting and hollering, a crowd assembled for the sake of hate—nothing could beat the mob mentality. It was great, and from an onlooker's perspective one would think they were having fun. But they *were* having fun. Lots of fun.

They were on their way to kill a family of niggers, on their way to slaughter a brother and a daughter and a mother and a father.

They started again and the mansion grew larger as they came closer. Up and over the hill. Across the bridge, the water underneath running wildly, splashing and splattering, fish jumping and jiving, one even diving over the bridge, circling the air and swishing into the water, no splash, no spray, the wooden posts creaking as feet stomped on over. The mob was getting closer.

The trees shrank out of view as they entered a field. It was nothing but grass for the rest of the way. Nathaniel held up his hand and the mob behind him all halted once more.

His brother, Bartholomew, turned and rode his horse the length of the mob, then turned and rode it the other way, as Nathaniel turned to face his faithful men and women. His mother was mad, and his father was madder.

Single-Mindlessness

Nathaniel, the maddest man and the most charismatic, said, "Tonight we force the niggers outta town. We show 'em their kind ain't wanted 'round here. They can pack up an' leave or be beheaded an' dismembered. This here is a white zone, only ordinary Christian folk allowed."

"HOORAH!!!"

More chanting and cheering and ranting and raving.

Nathaniel turned to face the mansion.

Then he went and the rest followed and his brother rode the horse on his right and his parents marched alongside. The sky was clear from here. No clouds up there, just a golden circle, or moreover, white and glowing. It wasn't gold, it was white. Showing the color of light.

The lights in the windows of the mansion flashed on and silhouettes bobbed into sight. Black shadows, big and small, a little girl's hair in a ponytail, and an even shorter boy's hair flat and tall. Their mother and father stood behind them.

The mob stopped again, and Nathaniel cupped his hands around his mouth and shouted, "Hey, you!!! You niggers!!! Leave or we comin' in after y'all!"

The silhouettes were still in the window.

"Now!!!"

The shadows dipped away and the creaking of the front door opening sounded from afar. Nathaniel stuck up his hand and the mob behind him stopped. He said something quiet to his brother, and the two of them started toward the mansion. The horse's hooves hit the ground in a steady gallop: not even a gallop, but strolling slowly. Nathaniel led and Bartholomew followed and the rest of the mob waited, curious, wondering what they were waiting

103

for, where the leaders were going, why the brothers made the mob stop and wait in the first place, and other such wonderings. It wasn't clear. From the looks of it one would think they went to barter with the niggers. Went to talk it through.

"Blasphemy," one muttered, and someone, out of the blue, shoved the man who muttered such a word to the ground, and a circle formed around the two men, who were rolling on the grass, fists pumping and plowing, punches sent barreling and jabbing, smashing and bashing. The man on top spoke—"You the blasphemous heathen!"—before his balled-up fists came down on the mutterer's head—"Not him, you!"—and again it cascaded—"Die, heathen, DIE!!!"—and the mutterer kicked to get free, but he couldn't and it only took one more hammer to the head—"That's right, DIE!!!"—before he submitted to the man on top. Cheering arose.

Cheering in honor of the man who'd snuffed the blasphemy.

It all had happened halfway to the back, and in the center of the mob the victor shouted, "If anyone try an' question our brillyant leaders again, a whoopin' awaits 'em"—he pranced around the fallen man, proud and showboating, pointing at the man who'd spoken such a treasonous word and had taken a pummeling to rid the mob of the poison he would sure promote.

The two brothers met the niggers. They spoke with them. From where they stood, the mob could hardly hear—their voices sounded muffled, the words unclear.

But they could see Bartholomew level the gun with the father's head. Nathaniel's hand, in a flash, tearing the sword from his sash and slashing at the mother's neck, but the sword suddenly stopping and the blade pressing into her skin. More muffled discussion. Then there sounded a bang and snapped a bright flash, and as the father fell to his knees, Nathaniel tore the sword through the mother's neck in an upward slant and her head dropped and rolled, blood spraying from the stump like a geyser. The two kids took off running, dashing through the darkness, toward the safety of their home. There followed two bangs and two bright flashes, and both kids went down flailing face-first into the grass.

The mob witnessed the violence from a distance and it seemed a spellbound silence had swept over them, jaws hanging limp, eyes wide and staring.

Nathaniel turned to face them, in his blood-stained overalls. Beside him his brother steered the horse around in a half-circle.

An awkward quiet pooled between the brothers and the mob. It was as though the mob didn't know what to do. The niggers were dead, so what now?

Suddenly Nathaniel lifted the sword high above his head and just simply screamed a deep, droning scream that went on and on as his brother's voice joined the cacophony of screaming.

Marge and Ralph started screaming as well.

Soon the mob caught on and they all hollered loudly and charged the mansion screaming.

It was a stampede of the righteous, with Nathaniel Helms and Bartholomew Helms way in the lead, Marge and Ralph Helms coming up close behind, and behind them swarmed a body of hatemongers, tearing through the field like a tidal wave.

That was how things went, Nathaniel and Bartholomew always far ahead of the rest, ever since they were kids, because their mom and dad had taught them well.

Their mom and dad, Marge and Ralph Helms, had taught them that the best way to obtain control was not through brute strength, but through sheer brainpower. Through mere intellect. Being the biggest and the baddest only got you so far, because once someone found a way to chain down the biggest and the baddest, they could turn him into a puppet. Into a murderous doll. A death machine doing its master's bidding.

Truth is, they didn't care much about race; it meant nothing to them. But what meant something was that Bartholomew's wife had been burned at the stake for being a witch, which she was not, and the whole town had watched and guffawed as the flames devoured her.

The black family was simply an easy target, a scapegoat, a catalyst that would set the wheels of hate in motion. Marge and Ralph had taught their two boys how to effectively round up a crowd, how to get the crowd on the same page—find a common cause for hate.

So there it happened: they riled up the town.

Marge and Ralph were so proud of their boys, for they couldn't have orchestrated this any better themselves.

In the commotion, Nathaniel and Bartholomew slowed to a walk as the mob shot past. It was like a tidal wave consuming a boulder protruding up from under the ocean, the boulder slipping through the liquid tyranny unscathed, the way the brothers were hit and then passed by the stampede.

They stopped and watched from a distance as the mob came to the mansion and set it aflame, the fire eating it up, spreading like a virus, and all the while they were smashing windows with the pitchforks and penetrating the door with the spiked tips. The doors and windows all broke down and the mob hurried inside and started breaking everything in sight. The fire grew and flickered. The townsfolk stole. The righteous men and women were cheering on the flames as they ripped the place apart, and soon struggled to breathe, the flames engulfing even them, and now they were ripping their way out, a block of wood plummeting and locking a man in, landing on his leg and crushing the bone. A woman ran to the door, a flame slashed at her, like whiplash, and thrashed once more, and she was stuck, dropping to her knees, her breathing ceasing.

More people were kicking and punching to get out, the flames devouring them like a fat man on Thanksgiving. The flames inevitably leaped from the walls, the ceiling, and the floorboards to the men and women of the mob, their skin bubbling and popping under the raw heat, pealing and dissipating, as if carrying a flesh-eating virus. Their blood boiled. Their bones fried, sizzling and crackling and crunching and crumbling into a pile.

The whole town went down in a smoldering blaze that night. All of them, except for the Helms family, who had watched it all happen through exuberant eyes. What a predictable lot, thought Bartholomew; their stupidity was their destruction. He let loose a deep belly laugh before Nathaniel gave him a victorious slap on the back. Bartholomew's head turned slightly and he glanced into his brother's eyes, the flickering flames of the evening dancing on their surfaces. Nathaniel nodded and his lips parted into a wide smile, a blood-thirsty grin that told Bartholomew everything he needed to know. They shared a brief moment that served as both comforting and reassuring, making it known that Nathaniel would do it again if he had to, and Bartholomew would do it too for Nathaniel if it came to that, and then the two brothers turned their backs on the burning mansion and walked away. Their parents turned too, but rather than follow, they stood there huddled beside each other, watching their two amazing sons walk off into the sunrise. A tear slipped down Marge's face, and Ralph leaned in and gave her a gentle kiss on the cheek. Then they fell in sync behind their two sons, leaving the flaming remains of the mansion to complete its path of destruction and the final screams of the night to fade....

Nefarious Endeavor #3

City: Boston, MA

Location: Logan Airport

It was the week before Christmas and people were getting ready to va-
cate to somewhere sunny and warm. Florida and California were two
hot spots. Anywhere south, really. Just to get out of the cold, snowy
north, is all these people wanted.

The bodily traffic was chest to back, chest to back, in the lines that
travelled through the security gates. People were taking off their shoes
and belts and storing them in the open boxes on the conveyor belt,

along with their carry-on luggage, and crossing through the metal-detectors and retrieving their items at the other end.

When Benny stepped through the metal-detector he was detected. He knew what it was that had set the detector off. It was the lock and chain he wore around his neck, for which he didn't have a key. The security detail knew this too, as he had forewarned them before crossing through, but still they insisted on patting him down.

"You have the option of going somewhere private," said the security guard.

"I'm fine," said Benny.

"You sure?" the man double-checked.

Benny glared at him in response.

"Okay, as you wish. Now, I am going to pat you down with the palms of my hands and use the backs in the more sensitive areas. Okay?"

Benny nodded.

"Good."

The security guard started moving his hands along the hem of Benny's waistband, and Benny felt a tinge of embarrassment. It sure was awkward having a grown man feel him up in public like this. He just didn't want to go off somewhere private for fear of what the man might do outside the view of the public.

Benny knew what could happen. In fact, he'd been victimized by authority in the past, and what made this instance any different? Benny didn't know. He tried to distract himself, but no good distractions arose. He tried, and he tried, but nothing presented itself.

Until the big-breasted brunette came jiggling through the detector.

Benny locked eyes on her, and smiled when the beep sounded and a beautiful uniformed black woman asked her to step aside. He looked forward to seeing her get patted down, so much in fact that he hoped she wouldn't ask to go somewhere private for the procedure.

"I'm going to move to the more sensitive areas now," said the security guard. "Hold up your pants, please."

Benny confirmed his instruction with a firm glance and gripped his waistband while watching the uniformed black woman mouth the same instructions Benny had gotten to the tall and slim toned woman with free-flowing brown hair and a great big smile. She replied, and

Benny saw the black woman weasel her fingers into the hem of the woman's tight but flexible waistband, wearing a grin that gleamed with irritation. But Benny was smiling, and he found it funny, the whole lot of the search procedure being imposed on this hot woman.

"Please stay here," the man searching Benny said.

Benny nodded.

The black woman then did the same to the rounded collar of the woman's shirt, which showed a decent amount of cleavage. She maneuvered her hands along the hem and over her breasts and then around her back.

"You're all set," the security guard said. "You may retrieve your luggage now."

Benny went and picked up the box containing his belt, wallet, a pocketful of change, his nostalgic dirt-stained Budweiser cap, and his cellphone. He brought his personal belongings over to a chair and set them down, then grabbed his shoes and his backpack and set those down beside the box.

Before putting everything back in their proper places, he turned and watched the woman being searched again, but the process had ended and the woman bent down over the conveyor belt, showing a voluptuous rump, and retrieved a box, and her purse, and a pair of high-heels, and strolled, like a runway model, to a chair across the way from Benny.

Her face showcased a look of disgust and outright annoyance, and Benny noticed a bright red light blink *inside* her right boob. That was odd.

But he saw it again.

And then ... *kaboom!!!*

A bright flash, a loud bang, and Benny was sent sprawling fifty feet backwards....

War Stories

A True Account

Names have been changed to protect the guilty.

ith a promise that I wouldn't drink until after the band recorded, I was bored. The band and I sat in my basement playing acoustically and discussing the upcoming recording session. We were to start at midnight, at Bernie's college, New England Institute of Art. Bernie was majoring in audio production. A year or two earlier I tried that same major at that same school but dropped out as soon as I'd decided I'd rather do coke.

My last day at NEiA (New England Institute of Art) I remember I'd carried a tinfoil wrapping of coke in my back pocket. Stiff Little Fingers had played that night in Brookline, and after class, since the school itself was in Brookline, I walked from there to the venue. My girlfriend Krissy was already there, carrying her bass case from the practice the previous day. We'd mistakenly sat behind a police station and blown the coke off the surface of her case.

It was a mistake because the surface was rough and pulling lines proved difficult. We'd probably wasted a bunch.

She wasn't in the band anymore. The last practice she'd attended was the one when I hurled my switchblade at our old drummer Stick Boy's younger sister. The blade missed her face by a few inches, and the blunt end punched a hole in the wall just above her head. One thing led to another, and Charlie, Krissy, and I piled into Charlie's pickup after I'd run a slash down her neck and she'd left in a huff and dialed the cops.

That was Stick Boy's last practice with us too.

Krissy left the band then but didn't yet leave me. That had happened when I'd run a knife through all four tires of her car.

She was gone now, and now I was dating Nicole from Cincinnati. Nicole was presently in Cincinnati visiting friends and family and was scheduled to arrive at Logan Airport the day after the recording session, at five AM. The band and I were to pick her up.

So it was Charlie, Matty, Jaded, and I now, all sitting in my basement waiting. Charlie played guitar, Jaded bass, and Matty drums. I sang. Unfortunately, since the house belonged to my parents, we had to smoke outside.

I remember one of those times the band and I got into an argument and I took off down the street. They must have searched all over for me. I wandered for a bit, until I heard hiphop coming from one of the houses. I took the liberty of going inside the house, and walked right into a party. The band had eventually found me there. They came through the door to find me pissing on the floor, surrounded by high school kids watching and looking pissed.

War Stories

They removed me from the situation, and I think the only reason no one took a swing at me or tried to stop me was because of the wooden baseball bat slung over my shoulder.

At some point in the night Dee Dee and two others joined us. One of the two was this guy whose name I don't remember, so for the sake of this story I'll call him Buddy. The other was a girl I'd never met before or even seen again. She looked different than all of us. Preppy. More put together. A picture was taken of the two of us in the bathroom.

The first time I remember meeting Dee Dee and Buddy was at a show in Arlington. We were told we were playing, so Predictable Chaos arrived there and it turned out it was a birthday party and we were not in fact playing. The bands that were playing were totally lame. They sucked, and we started these mosh pits that the adults tried to stop. Charlie chucked a chair at the crowd. It hit the ground with a clang. When the band onstage finished their set, the four of us in Predictable Chaos climbed up there and hijacked their gear. We hijacked the show and played a short set before the cops were called and we had to go.

That was where I met Dee Dee and Buddy.

Though I don't recall why they were at our recording session and who called them and invited them to come. Bernie had made it very clear that we were to show up alone, just Charlie, Matty, Jaded, and I.

I promised him we wouldn't drink, and the band promised me the same, yet I showed up with a pint of whiskey in my inside jacket pocket and snuck off between songs to take a swig. This irritated the band. We ended up fighting because I was piss drunk and they were not.

119

I took out my anger by slamming that wooden bat into every-thing in sight. Signs. Cars. Parking meters. This one sign shat-tered, and in the wake of the bat was an outline of what looked like a face. I snapped a picture of it.

In the end the recordings came out like crap, and I believe Ber-nie scratched them, the asshole that he was. Our earlier record-ings, done in an actual studio, also sounded like crap; well, I sup-pose they weren't so bad, just sounded two-dimensional because we ran out of money to finish them up and the guy responsible for recording ripped us off—he charged too much.

At the studio, in the bathroom, Krissy and I met this fat old guy with a gut protruding out from under his white T-shirt. The old guy told us if we were to do coke, something we had blown quite frequently in those days, we ought to not be drunk, because then the coke would only sober us up. So from that we resigned to only drinking beer before we did blow.

Although drinking harder liquor was a must when I was out with Charlie because if I wanted him to buy for us we had better be drunk.

Charlie spent his whole life savings on the two of us. Every night he would resign to not buying any more coke, but when the bottle was halfway gone I'd turn to him and suggest we go and get some. He would go, Hmm, and I would go, Yes, let's do it, and he would go, Hmm, and I would finally say, Come on, get off your ass and let's get some crack.

The recording session that night was a bust and all seven of us, not including Bernie, piled into Matty's car like a band of clowns. He drove us to Logan and I spotted Nicole there.

War Stories

Nicole was my girlfriend. The night I slashed Krissy's tires was the night I met her, though it wasn't that simple. She met Charlie first, and the two of them hooked up. They staggered up to me, while I leaned against the wall outside the Middle East, drunk. Charlie introduced us. Her name was Nicole.

Later on, I got jumped by a couple of wiggers. I thought they were trying to hook up with Krissy, so I challenged them to a fight in the parking lot where we stood. This happened after I'd verbally assaulted a cop.

Krissy broke up the commotion and took off somewhere down the street. I drunkenly tried to follow, but lost her rather quick, and next thing a flash zipped out of the alleyway and charged me head-on. It looked like a flash because my vision was gone. From nowhere something slammed into my head. It caught me off guard and I stumbled and tripped and landed on my back. Before long two guys were grounding their shoes into my prone body. They were stomping me, and my phone broke loose and rolled to a stop a few feet from me. I lunged for it and picked it up.

The following day I realized it wasn't mine, and Krissy called my landline and told me that when she called my phone someone named Nicole picked up. So I arranged to meet Nicole later that day at the Fenway train station, and we switched back the phones.

Again, a month or two later, we ran into Nicole at a Predictable Chaos show. And, again, she and Charlie hooked up. We went back to her dormitory at three in the morning and I rapped my knuckles on each and every door on our way to her room. We went into the bathroom and had a toilet paper party, and I climbed onto the door and sat there as a girl stepped out of the shower stall wrapped in a towel. Upon seeing us she ducked back into the stall and cowered there until we left.

We went back to her room and trashed the place. I put on one of her skirts and her fishnet tights and ran lipstick along my lips. They took a picture of me. We trashed the place, and in the morning waited outside the liquor store for it to open. When we went back to her dorm, she kicked us out after having a bitch attack. Later on, Charlie told me she said she would never in a million years hook up with me because I was a scumbag. Jamie had told her that.

Last time I'd seen Jamie, I went to this kid's birthday party and beforehand promised I would not drink. When I got there I saw Karen and some guy drinking beneath the bridge. I joined them down there and took a couple swigs, then was met outside the party by Jamie, who kind of attacked me and wrung my neck. Karen and the guy told Jamie I hadn't drunk any. Seriously, he hadn't drunk any, they said. Charlie arrived later and even later we went to Maggie's apartment and shot coke with Maggie.

Since Nicole thought I was a scumbag and for that reason she wouldn't even fuck me with someone else's cunt, I took the liberty of calling her some days later, and it only took a week before we hooked up. I'd made her mine on the coldest night that winter, I remember. We got on the train so that Nicole could get off at Fenway, where her college was, and I could get off at Newton Highlands, where I lived all my life. We met this kid about our age, maybe older, on the train. He was a Punk rock kid all decked in spikes and studs, and he invited us back to his place to drink more and smoke bud. We were on the last train already, so if we were to get off, we'd be stranded out in Boston for the night. So we could stay at his place, he said. No problem.

Although his girlfriend called and was coming over, so we had to go at about one in the morning. We were cold and stranded. We walked back to the train tracks, where we figured we'd wait out the night, probably die from the cold. But on the way Nicole pointed out to me a backdoor left askew, and on that note we were over the fence and slipping into the insulated basement in no time, although it was so cold out we could feel it inside. All the heaters were down there, and we could hear them buzzing and rattling the entire night. A loud racket came from above, people screaming and stomping feet, and we laughed at that and cuddled with each other to keep warm. I took a piss in the corner, without realizing we were lying on a slant, and the piss streamed under us as we made out on the cold, hard floor. The next day we both smelt like piss.

At Logan Airport I stepped out of Matty's car and waved Nicole over, and she joined us inside and Matty drove us back to my house. On the way we picked up some wine and got drunk all over again.

Jeremy Void

A Shitty Short Story

A **guy has to take** a shit really bad while at the grocery store buying a pack of smokes. The feeling of having to shit has come out of nowhere and it hurts more than anything. He ditches out of the line briskly and heads for the bathroom, walking congested as though a pole is speared up his butthole. He gets to the men's room, enters, and, unfortunately, there are only two stalls and both are occupied. He waits for one to open. It takes too long. He decides to use the ladies' room instead, which he finds to contain four stalls, one of which is occupied, the one closest to the far wall, and he uses the stall closest to the door. The shit won't come out easily. When it finally does, he feels his skin tearing and thinks he's going to die, that his intestines are going to be ripped out in the process, with the release of the shit. He pushes, feels a burning in his anus, goes light-headed, and hears a plop and knows it's over. As he reaches beneath him to wipe he feels something sharp bite down on his hand. When he retrieves his hand a lizard's jaw is clamped to it, and he faints.

Jeremy Void

Bloody Harry
A Tribute to Hubert Selby, Jr.

①————Harry punched his employee ID in the touchscreen computer, clocking out of work. As he left the bank he said goodbye to all his coworkers.

"Bye, Harry," was the general consensus as he exited through the first set of doors and entered a small room where the ATM machine was and exited through the second set of doors, squinted at the sun as he slid his dark glasses over his ears, and started down Merchant's Row, in Rutland, Vermont.

A big smile suspended his cheekbones, and to the passersby he was glowing. He tipped his hat to a beautiful brunette in a tight miniskirt and sexy suit jacket. She smiled back.

He stepped out of the searing heat into the Coffee Exchange, located at the corner of Merchant's Row and Main Street, and approached the counter. The familiar clerk smiled. She was a young lady with long blond hair and blue eyes and had slender curves that caught Harry's eyes each and every time he came in.

"Hi, Harry," she said through that beautiful smile of hers.

131

"Mariah, nice to see you."

"Nice to see you too. Now, what can I get you?"

"A medium light roast in a to-go cup, please."

She picked up a cup from the stack beside the register and marched off to the coffee and pushed down on the lever and coffee streamed out the nozzle and into the cup.

"Room for cream?" she asked loud enough so Harry could hear from where he stood.

"Yes, please."

She brought back the cup and steam wafted up and the marquee looming over the register read $2.00, and Mariah reiterated the cost incase Harry hadn't taken note of it. Harry obliged, passing two crisp one-dollar bills to Mariah, along with a card with three little holes punched in a row and seven spots awaiting a punch so that Harry could treat himself to a free barista drink.

After setting the cash in the drawer Mariah punched the fourth hole in the card and passed it back over the counter. Harry tipped his hat to her, in a way of saying thanks, and sidled over to the milk and sugar station, where he probably poured too much milk in the cup and added a heavy serving of sugar, then stirred the concoction with a thin black straw before discarding the straw in the garbage.

He glanced back over to Mariah, and she was occupied mixing an espresso drink with the barista machine at the moment.

He found a seat at a tall table, the chair rather tall too. He had to lift himself off his tippy toes just to sit. He set the drink on the table and watched as customers streamed through the door in waves, one every now and then, and a heavy flow every few minutes or so. Customers of only two different genders, and of only a few breeds, similar-looking people with slightly different facial features, teenagers dressed in hipster getups, having just gotten out of school, and adults dressed up nice, having just gotten off work and wanting to grab a coffee before going home and getting ready to go back out and hop from one bar to the next. There were young adults in the mix too, wielding laptop cases or book bags, typing away on their computers or reading books or writing in notebooks. All in all, this was Rutland, Vermont, and color was uncommon. A rarity, but not an impossibility.

Harry, in fact, daydreamed about different sorts coming through that door, watching each and every customer in hope that one would differ from the rest. But nobody ever strayed too far from the norm. Nobody would take that chance, not in Rutland, of all places. God, Harry wished he could pack up and go on leave to Boston for only just a week and see all the various customs, the cultural differences, those who were unafraid to stand out. Harry, too, was scared to do just that. He worked in a respectable business, and couldn't afford to isolate himself from his coworkers.

Harry's smile faltered at the hopelessness of his thinking.

Although then something strange took place.

A young lady, eighteen or older, strode through the door. She had a tall purple Mohawk, the likes of which Harry had never seen. Her black jeans were fitted tight and she wore a sleeveless white shirt showing a sleeve of tattoos on her right arm. The shirt was cut into a V-neck, clearly done herself, and a couple of rips showed some skin and an inch of her purple bra. Harry was immediately intrigued by this woman. He watched her walk to the counter, in utter awe at the way she carried herself, so smooth and in control. Now, *she* was colorful.

She ordered an iced mocha latte and took the drink to a round table and sat all alone. Out of her purse she pulled a book and opened it and delved into the words on the page, and Harry watched her read, so in tune with it, lost in the colorful world of fiction. He wanted nothing more than to know what she was reading, but felt an innate fear of approaching this woman, for what if she rejected him, or made him look like a clown? No, not a clown, but a fool.

A fool for thinking someone like her would want to talk to someone like Harry, someone from such a different world, and he watched her flip the page and sip her drink and delve into the words again.

❷——Harry lived a simple life, had his own apartment on Prospect Street, and had a couple of close friends, or moreover, acquaintances who would join him Friday nights at the Downtown Tavern, and they would get good and drunk, and every now and then Harry would meet a nice girl and bring her home and they would rush through the door, and inside, and hurry to Harry's bedroom and Harry would push her smack dab in the center of his bed, an act of drunken lust, and dive on top of the girl, and they would kiss and roll and mess up the bedspread, and soon Harry would breech her private parts with his hard rocket, and she would twist and turn, and scream and moan, and Harry would huff and puff, panting as the rocket shot. Then he would nurture his hangover the next day with a warm cup of coffee, and would always make the nice girl breakfast, eggs and bacon, a Saturday morning ritual. He would spend the remainder of his weekends at home or at the gym, watching movies on the TV or working his muscles violently, running on the treadmill while listening to the Red Sox game on the radio, via headphones.

Then Monday morning would come, and he'd shower, get dressed, and go to work, and all his coworkers would smile as he strode through the door.

That was Harry's life.

③——The following day, after leaving the bank, Harry hoped to see Purple—an alias he'd given her because he didn't know her true name—again at the Coffee Exchange. But she didn't show. So he came back the next day and waited and waited, and he waited, but she didn't show, so he came back again. A month went by and Harry sat disappointed at the Coffee Exchange, and when he was about to give up, the door opened and Purple came in.

Harry watched as she ordered a drink and sat at the same round table. This time he caught the title of the book she took out of her purse—*Last Exit to Brooklyn*—but missed the author's name as she opened it up and dove into the words.

She seemed really into the book, and Harry wrote a note to himself to go next door and browse for said book. He finished his coffee, tossed it in the trash, and Purple caught his glance, with a roll of her eyes, as he stepped out into the heat and shaded his eyes with his dark sunglasses. Through the window, as he started down the street, he stole one more peek at Purple, then veered left into the Book King.

The woman working there seemed nice enough when Harry asked if she carried *Last Exit to Brooklyn*.

"Never heard of it," she said.

Harry frowned, waving goodbye and saying thanks anyway as the heat from outside exploded in his face like a bonfire exploding and expanding when you drop a large branch littered with dead leaves into the flames.

Harry jammed his hands into his pant pockets and peered at his feet, moping as he climbed the street and headed home.

Monday ended when he passed out on his bed and dreamed of meeting Purple.

Like that would happen.

He would never meet her in person, he knew, because she was so peculiar, whereas he was way too normal, too quant, as his coworkers would say.

❹——Tuesday, Wednesday, and Thursday passed like a cargo train, and Friday came and went, Harry's drawer falling short at the end of the day.

"You're off by forty dollars," his boss hollered, pacing in front of his desk. He was a big man, bald and tan, with a gut that jutted out and hung over his waistband. When he was mad a vein running the length of his head would pulse and throb. Right now he was mad. He stopped his senseless pacing and looked straight into Harry's blank face—a face flushed with no emotions, for Harry's mind was elsewhere, unable to stop thinking about Purple, whoever she was.

"I must have made a mistake," Harry pleaded, and he looked like a child who'd been caught stealing a cookie off the counter of a coffee shop, sweat darkening the armpits of his white button-down shirt.

He reached into his back pocket to remove his wallet and pay back what he owed, but thankfully his boss was a reasonable man, holding up his hand and saying, "It's okay."

"You sure?"

"This is the first time you screwed up like this, so yes, I'm sure." An awkward pause, then: "And it better be the last," he added.

"Thank you," Harry said, tipping his hat to show his gratitude.

He felt relieved as he left the bank, passing an old man talking to himself as he played with the ATM machine, as if it were a slot machine.

⑤———He went and did what he'd done these recent Fridays after work, and that was to sit at the coffee shop and hope Purple would walk in, and she did, her purple hawk combed to the side and hanging in front of her right eye.

What the hell, Harry thought, and got up and walked nervously to Purple, who was seated at the table reading a different book. "Mind if I sit down?" Harry asked politely, pulling out a chair.

She shrugged nonchalantly and went back to reading the book.

She didn't say yes, but neither did she say what he'd expected—*No, you can't,* he'd thought she'd say, then sneer at him for the attempt, and he would walk away with his tail wagging between his legs. But that was not what had happened and he took that as his cue to plop in the chair across from her and say his name was Harry. She peered over the book, almost investigating him, reading him as if he himself were the book she was so infatuated with.

"Sherry," she said.

"Nice to meet you." He reached his hand over the table, and this time she did sneer, though not at him, but at the idle hand raised before her face.

"Hi," she said, and again went back to the book.

"So," Harry started, trying to provoke some kind of talk between the two of them. "What's with the purple hair?"

She peered over the pages and smirked.

"I'm getting up," Harry said.

"No," she replied immediately. "I'm sorry, it's just people like … well, people like you look down upon people like me. For example, 'What's with the purple hair?' I mean, for fuck's sake, what do you care? Do you even care? Or are you just here to make fun of me like all your buddies I'm sure would do?"

Harry was taken aback by that response.

"So what is it, then?"

"Uh…." Harry didn't have a response at first, couldn't conjure up the right words. "I don't have any buddies."

"Ha!" The singular laugh seemed fake but real at the same extent. "You mean to tell me you have no friends?"

"I have acquaintances."

"And what would they think of you talking to someone like me?"

"They wouldn't approve, but that's just Rutland for you. I mean, you even from around here?"

"No." She stopped at that and resumed her reading.

"What book are you reading?"

She showed him the cover, and Harry read the words—*American Skin* by Don De Grazia—and nodded. "Are you a skinhead?"

"In a way I guess you could say so."

"Then what's with the Mohawk?"

"It's called a Chelsea-hawk—it would be more identifiable with my hair charged up, but that basically means a Mohawk with the bangs kept, as a Chelsea cut, something the girl skinheads would have, is a short-trimmed haircut with the bangs still there."

Harry nodded, having a hard time understanding, as if she were speaking some foreign tongue.

"Don't worry about trying to understand," she said, knowing well that he couldn't even if he wanted to, for you had to be part of the scene to fully get it.

"So where you from?"

"What is this, the third degree?"

"No, I'm just curious."

She sighed. "Lived on Staten Island in New York, New York, for a while, then at eighteen I moved to Boston, where I met my boyfriend, and sick of the drama that comes with city life, he and I came to Rutland." She stopped for a moment. "And," she added, "boy, did we make a mistake."

"Then why not leave?"

"We're broke."

"Too many drugs?"

"What?" she snarled.

"I'm sorry," Harry said, not truly remorseful for what he had said. These Punk rock girls were always strung out on something, Harry knew for a fact.

She held up her hands and showed him the backs. "See those Xs tattooed on each hand?"

Harry nodded. "Yeah, but what about them?"

"That means I don't drink, do drugs, or even partake in premarital sex, which drives my boyfriend bonkers. But he loves me and is willing to put up with it whether he likes it or not."

Harry's brows furrowed. Then he regretfully said, "Want to join me for lunch tomorrow, right after I leave the gym, go home, shower and change? I'll pick you up."

He saw the forlorn in her eyes, and knew what would come next, but was quite surprised when she said, "Yes." She said, "Why not?"

Harry smiled a smile like the smile he'd smiled the first day he saw her come in, but hadn't felt so strongly about anything since, until now.

"Really?" he chirped, then cleared his throat. "I mean"—in a much more manly tone—"where do you live?"

"Meet me here."

And with that she took her coffee and left.

But Harry never made clear what time he would pick her up.

6——Saturday morning came with a bright sun beaming through his window and then the shade and burning a design, the shape and size of the window, on the floor in his bedroom.

He awoke dreary-eyed but cheery and stretched out his arms as he yawned with magnificent force. He awoke alone this morning, as he had skipped a night at the bar for excitement at the thought of seeing Sherry again and going on a—sort of—date. He went into the kitchen and cooked himself up a batch of eggs and bacon, then rushed out the door and hurried to the Coffee Exchange for an early-morning appearance, which he never did, especially not on a Saturday, and he sat there all day, without even thinking

140

about the gym or about abandoning his routine for a girl he'd only just met, but he knew something was special about her, maybe just the fact that she brought color to an otherwise colorless existence which was Harry's life.

He waited and waited for her to show, and checked his watch at noon, and then waited another hour before she finally came through the door.

She greeted him with a warm smile as he sipped the cold coffee he had ordered when he first got there.

"Can I get you anything?" he asked.

"It's all right," she said. "I have money."

"No, really, I insist."

She groaned, then said, "An iced mocha latte," and added, "Thank you so much … Harry, right?"

"Yeah, Harry." He felt neglected at the thought of her already forgetting his name.

"Sorry," she said surprisingly. "My memory's not all that great."

"From the drugs?" he said impulsively, seeming eager to get it off his chest.

She growled, grinding her teeth. "I thought," she said through gritted teeth, "I told you I was straight edge."

"Right." He got up and went to the counter, and Emily was working there. She looked similar to Mariah, only she was taller and had longer hair, a shimmering shade of brown, and Harry knew she'd seen him checking her out as she passed, but he also knew she felt acknowledged by this so just ignored it because the two of them were well acquainted from Harry's many visits to the Coffee Exchange.

"An iced mocha latte," he said, handing over his empty coffee cup, "and a refill, please."

She filled the order and rang him up, and, holding two steaming cups in his hand, he went back to where Sherry sat talking on her phone, arguing with someone, possibly her boyfriend, saying it was none of his business who she chose to hang out with, then hung up with intense emotions and sighed as Harry set her drink down.

"Your boyfriend?"

"Yeah," she said. "How'd you know?"

Harry shrugged, this time him acting all nonchalant, before sipping his coffee and making eye contact with Sherry.

"First of all, Harry"—he nodded as she continued—"you seem like a nice guy and all, but I still wanna lay it down on the table that no matter what you think is going on, I have no intentions of hooking up with you, as I love my boyfriend"—she said it slowly so as not to be misinterpreted—"so don't think otherwise!" The last four words had come out very strongly, and Harry wondered what her real intents were, as she wouldn't be laying this out so early if she had absolutely no interest in making love to him—*Love*, was how he said it in his head, because ever since he'd first laid eyes on Sherry, he'd been falling fast in love, and if she only knew, which he was almost certain she did.

They talked and joked and laughed, some of the jokes borderline sexual, which gave Harry a jolt in his crotch, and they said goodbye and even hugged, before she left through the door and he slumped back down in the chair, so deeply in love with this girl, so taken aback by how good things had been going, so much better and moving so much quicker than Harry had even expected. He

Bloody Harry

was sure that on their third date it would be made official and they would fuck all night long and Harry would make her eggs and bacon and they would eat together and she would leave and say she couldn't wait to see him again.

Daydream, was what Harry did, and continued to do until Tuesday, when the two of them met at the Coffee Exchange again and this time exchanged numbers, and a day later he phoned her and asked if she wanted to go down to Pub 42, but she said no. "Harry, I told you I don't drink." He then said, "That's okay, you don't have to. I'll do all the drinking for you," and she laughed at that and sighed and said, "Okay, I'll be there in half an hour."

To that Harry smiled, a bit benignly, but still a smile of joy.

⑦———Tonight at Pub 42, by Harry's account, was their third date, and they danced together and laughed at each other's jokes—this girl just loved to laugh and make others around her laugh too, Harry knew and took advantage of the fact, cracking jokes every chance he could get—and when the bartender made an announcement that right now was the last call for alcohol, Harry whispered in her ear: "Come back to my place and continue the night there."

She said okay, and the two of them left and went to Harry's, and Harry smoked weed as she ate pizza, and amid all the fun they were having, Harry asked the long awaited question, the elephant in the room:

"Are you faithful to your boyfriend?"

A look of fright shattered her smile, the smile she'd worn all night, and she very quickly said yes, without even a moment's thought, a beat not having passed, and Harry knew if he kept pursuing she would soon concede.

143

Which was why two nights later at one a.m. he called her phone, and he called and called and hoped to go on a hike with her, but not even a single remark came from the other end, not even a *Harry, I'm sleeping,* so he called some more, the goal to arouse her awake and bring her out to the woods and set up a picnic blanket and the two of them would look up at the stars, and in that moment of romance, the two of them lying on their backs, she would roll over onto Harry and make the first move, which Harry knew would come, and they would kiss and roll and mess up the blanket spread out on the sand, and soon Harry would breech her private parts with his hard rocket, and she would twist and turn, and scream and moan, and he would huff and puff, panting as the rocket shot. And from the cues he was receiving from her, via body language, he knew for a fact that she would want to come back and dump her boyfriend's sorry ass, and she would be Harry's, and only his, and he could claim her as his own, and as he hit redial, praying to God that she would answer so he could tell her about the events he'd planned to partake in with her this evening, his dick rose an inch and then rose some more.

But she didn't pick up, and Harry set the phone down on the bedside table and decided to call it a night.

Bitch, Harry thought.

8———Later that same day, Friday afternoon, he got a text message from her that said she was scared about how he'd kept calling so late at night and he promised it would never happen again, although he knew it would, not tonight or tomorrow night, but he knew what she wanted—no, what she needed, and he was very, very willing to give it to her. He knew she just needed a good fuck as all girls did, and he knew once after, she would have fallen for him like he'd fallen for her.

⑨——The day soon came when they met at the Coffee Exchange and a frown disfigured her otherwise beautiful face.

"What's wrong?" Harry asked her, feigning concern, but he already knew the problem—she'd broken up with her boyfriend to be with him and a surge of emotional, electric energy made his dick stir and start to rise. He smiled and said, "Don't worry, everything will be fine."

Her frown turned into something of surprise and he saw it in her eyes that he was wrong by a long shot and he asked again, "What's wrong?"

"It's my boyfriend," she said. Harry was excited by this but didn't want her to know, so just continued to play the game.

"I'm sorry." He again pretended to be the loving and caring guy he himself knew she deserved, but also knew he didn't give two shits about her boyfriend anymore, nor did he her, but only wanted one thing, and that one thing was giftwrapped inside those sexy tight black pants.

"About what, Harry?"

"Uh…." He fucked up and he knew it. "What's wrong with your boyfriend?"

"He can be such a jealous asshole at times."

His pants, he could feel, were tightening at the thought of this cretin being jealous of Harry of all people, that he was threatened by Harry presence, but oh no, nothing would happen, nothing that she didn't want, anyway. He had a right to feel jealous, and if Harry were her boyfriend he'd come at Harry with a pipe and pound that sorry smile off his face. *Shit,* Harry thought, for he didn't even know anything about Sherry's asshole boyfriend; he could be a big football player for all he—

"Harry!" she shouted.

"What?"

"What's the matter with you? You're just staring off into space while I'm talking to you. Snap the fuck out of it."

He surged up to give her his undivided attention.

"He doesn't want me to hang around you anymore. Says you sound like a creep. But I disagree, Harry, you seem harmless. And besides, I think I could take you if you acted out of line."

He hoped she would, rolling around on the floor, wrestling, as some would call it, which he was sure would turn into what he was after—that being a quick bang and a leave of absence without telling her anything about where he went, as after the way she'd treated him, she deserved nothing more.

"Would you like me to talk to him?" he said with a sly smile.

"I don't know, Harry."

"It's okay, I'll be nice."

"Trust me when I say, I'm not worried about him, but I am very worried about what he might do to you, for he stabbed this dude six times the size of him because the dude tried to kiss me and after saying no maybe five or six times I gave in, and he thrust a steak knife into the dude's thick neck. My boyfriend, trust me on this, is a high-tension wire."

"He doesn't sound too safe," Harry said, internally laughing at the prospect of Sherry taking Harry's side and eventually going home with Harry, and the thought made his dick start to rise again. "It doesn't sound at all safe for you to be going with him."

"He would never hurt me; he loves me."

"Then maybe you could tell him it would pain you to see him beat on me," Harry told her. He just wanted to meet this fuck somewhere and give him some of his own medicine.

"Harry, please." She stopped, stalled, then turned and said over her shoulder: "I'm outta here."

This comment brewed anger inside the darkest corner of Harry's mind, and his eyes showed the rage, and as Emily passed to deliver a drink and came back his way, she asked if he was okay, and he said he was fine. He lied to her, and something about that felt good, like a thrill he'd never before experienced, living darkly and dishonest, something only a Punk rocker could turn a man into, and he blamed her even though he enjoyed this abnormal hate that festered inside; he liked it a lot and wanted to feel more of it.

⑩——Then days went by without seeing Sherry again, and after two weeks he called her landline in hope her boyfriend would answer, and he did.

"Hello?"

"Who's this?" Harry asked, with a grin that couldn't be seen on the other side of the phone line, which made the secrecy of his thoughts feel almost romantic.

"You called me, asshole," her boyfriend snarled.

Harry chuckled, muffling the mouthpiece so he couldn't hear his demonic laughter. But Harry sure could hear it and hear it he did; the pleasure of death twisted and tortured and forced into his head by an evil Punk rock chick made him feel more alive than ever.

"Who the fuck is this????"

"Harry." He coughed. "It's Harry, you fuck. And I want you to stop seeing Sherry."

"You want *me* to stop seeing her? Who the fuck do you think you are??"

"Your worst nightmare."

"How original."

Harry jammed his thumb into the END button as hard as he could, and then when he tried calling Sherry on her cell, he got nothing, not even a dial tone, but an unsettling blankness, Harry stuck with his own fucked-up thoughts, and he couldn't take it.

He threw his jacket on over his shoulders and stormed down the street and kept going until he reached the Downtown Tavern, and once there he ordered a beer, and then another, and then another, and when he saw the drunken grin on the biggest motherfucker there, who had two girls wrapped in his arms, he walked over and hurled his fist, packed with a roll of quarters, and the big bruiser went splat on the ground, and Harry left the bar, leaving the patrons and his so-called friends, or acquaintances, in utter shock of what had proceeded here this evening, and in a wondering disbelief at what had gotten into their very pacifist friend, who had, as far as they knew, never been in one single fight his whole life, and now this ... *what the hell had happened????*

Harry arrived home and fell asleep with ease on his bed, dreaming of meeting that squirrely boyfriend of Sherry's and damaging the already damaged punk by doing what he had done to the big man downtown, and then he could laugh, and in his sleep he laughed, though nobody heard, for he lived alone, but not for long, as he was sure Sherry would want to move in in the near future, for she loved him, he knew, but she wasn't yet willing to take her love to such an extreme, or even concede to those strong emotions that might be confusing to her right now.

But he knew those emotions were there, and when he woke up that morning he felt a new sense of pride and felt like he could in fact break the norms set by those before him and followed out by those who rotted away in the Rut.

The first thing he did that morning was open a drawer and pull out his clippers and run them along his head, followed by a Bic razor that would shave his head completely clean of the fuzz leftover from the clippers, and what he did was more out of rage than a sense of self, feeling like a change was prudent at present, so he walked out of the bathroom a changed man and went to work looking like a mess, in jeans and a white T-shirt, a few knife slits in the white fabric.

Today he could tell was different, as nobody said hello, but instead stared like they'd seen a ghost, but maybe they had, the ghost of Harry, who lurked Citizens Bank and popped open his drawer, quickly pocketing the cash, and while the man in charge screamed some sense into Harry, he immediately left the bank and called Sherry again and then raised the ringing phone to his ear.

"What do you want, Harry?"

"WHAT????" he snapped.

"Harry, what's gotten into you?"

"You, my dear, and now it's my turn to get into you."

"Harry, please, calm down."

This new sense of rage, of hate, that he felt, this urgent sense to destroy what he hated and take what he wanted from those who deserved nothing else—it filled him with joy and a newfound reason to live.

He glared at all the passersby and they stepped out of his path, well aware of what might occur if they crossed him the wrong way, and he thrived on that fear he instilled in all those fucking drones, enslaved to jobs they could care less about, but continued to go to because they needed the pay that came at the end of each week, and Harry knew they were just whores, and he was once a whore too, but no more would he whore himself to the corporate machine.

He marched down the street with purpose and entered the door to the Coffee Exchange and very rudely ordered a mocha latte for the lady.

But what lady? Emily and Mariah both wondered, worried about what had changed. He took the drinks from them and again marched with purpose straight out the door, neglecting to give even a dime to those cheap whores—fucking minimum-wage sluts.

Emily chased him out and when she caught up he rammed his palm into her plastic face and laughed when she sank to her butt, clearly in pain. Harry turned and walked away.

He went straight home and ran a reverse search on the online White Pages for where Sherry lived, and printed out her address, and as she didn't live too far, she and her boy toy, he began walking in the direction of her house.

⑪——While standing in front of Sherry's apartment he shouted, "Hey!"

Sherry peered out the window at him. She slid open the frame and asked what he wanted.

"I just want to talk," he said calmly, cupping his hand around his mouth to project the words straight to her.

"Okay, I'll be right down."

Bloody Harry

And she was down in an instant, and Harry instantly back-handed her across the face with such force that she stumbled away. Standing in the doorway, her boyfriend saw from a distance and then stormed through the door.

"What the fuck!!!" he shouted, in a challenging manner, and ran at Harry.

But little did he know, Harry had a surprise up his sleeve, a hidden knife that slid up his wrist and out of his sleeve and sliced open Sherry's boyfriend's throat so quick and violently that Sherry was frozen in shock.

Then he went at Sherry and insisted in a calm, reassuring voice that it might be wise of her right now to spread her legs and show Harry the love he was well aware that she felt.

She crab-walked in the opposite direction, screaming as loud as she could: "Rape! Rape!"

"No one can hear your futile cries for help," Harry said. "But fuck 'em, right? What're they gonna do? Call the cops?" He pulled a 9mm Glock out of his waistband and cocked it, and a spare shell flew out and landed on the grass, and Harry smiled psychotically, his facial expression bordering something socio-pathic, but he didn't care, well aware of how he looked.

"Have you seen yourself lately, Harry?" Sherry tried to hammer sense into his head. "Have you looked in the mirror? What happened to that nice guy I met months ago?"

"You happened to him," he said, and aimed the pistol at her head.

"Harry," she cooed in a soft, loving voice. "You don't have to do this."

"I know." And his smile only widened as he put slight pressure on the trigger and saw Sherry's eyes squeeze shut and saw the tears seeping out the corners. It was then when he realized he'd been possessed. These actions weren't his own. How could they be, being the nice and gentle guy that he was? He dropped to his knees and started to sob uncontrollably, his shoulders bouncing sporadically.

"Harry, it's okay," Sherry said as she stood up and went over to him and rubbed his back soothingly.

"But it's not okay," Harry cried out. "It's not. You don't deserve any of this. Any of what I put you through." He raised the gun to his head and squeezed the trigger, and just as police cruisers sped down the street toward the madness, Harry stained Sherry's white shirt with his brains and plopped on the ground, blood spilling out the large hole in his head and forming a bloody puddle by her feet. She cried as the cops exited their cruiser and came over to comfort her. She even vomited, adding to the puddle the dinner she'd eaten with Ron, her boyfriend, who also lay dead on the grass, and her whole life was out of control, and she cried and cried, and a cop put his arm around her back and led her to the backseat of his cruiser. She sat there with the door open, halfway out and halfway in, and one of the cops brought her a cup of coffee, which she sipped slowly, fighting back tears, which soon poured from her eyes as she shook out of sheer misery of what had gone on, and what she had created, even though later in a therapy session with her court-appointed grief counselor, the overly empathetic woman assigned to her case assured her that none of this was her fault.

But she knew the truth, and she bullshitted the counselor, telling her she knew it wasn't her fault....

Nefarious Endeavor #4

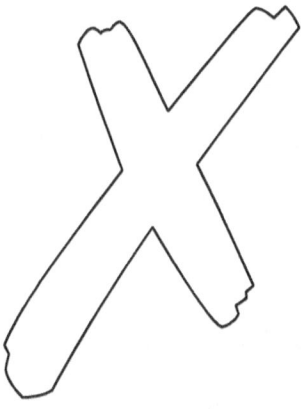

Judy slid a quarter into the juke, two quarters, three, four; she flipped
a few dials, pushed a couple buttons. An upbeat synthesized drumbeat thumped while Judy jerked her rump, methodically, to the
rhythm, with the tapping of her left foot, her knee bending, her butt
bumping. A synthesized guitar chimed in moments later—Iggy Pop's
"Lust for Life"—and she turned and faced the bar, eased her eyes
shut, and her legs were jumping, and she was running sideways, side
to side, seesawing, her head weaving and waving and swirling, her hair
fanning and the individual strands separating like tiny tentacles, as
though electric.

Her dancing grabbed the attention of the bar, and three big red-necks and one cowboy wannabe-type swiveled on their stools. They were all cheering. Leering. One even yelled, "Take off your clothes."

Judy was an angel, her movements graceful and methodic and hot. She was lost. She didn't hear the redneck yell. To her the cheering and chanting and ranting and raving came from the tune playing on the juke.

She swirled, bobbed, dipped, and dropped to her knees, folding, her back almost touching the floor, her stomach bending, and she rose up and the show recommenced—or did it ever stop?

In her head, behind closed lids, she saw an array of rhythmic flashes, sharp colorful shapes striking the black, a fireworks show be-hind closed eyes. She was having a blast. The rednecks didn't exist. She was alone, alone, alone in her own head, in her own thoughts, lost in the music.

It was all good clean fun, so much fun, until she felt five fingers clench her butt; the gunshot was loud. Judy opened her eyes, and by her feet was a dead redneck, his head blown clean off, and at the bar sat the cowboy wannabe-type pointing a sawed-off shotgun her way. He smiled.

Her hands, with surreal speed, ripped two butterfly knives from her waistband, swirled them open, and hurled them both simultaneously at one of the remaining rednecks. The two blades tore through each peck. A small six-shooter hidden in Judy's boot, she fetched and fired and the bullet sank between his eyes.

Kev, her boyfriend, the killer cowboy, with a murderous grin, turned and squeezed the trigger. An onslaught of shrapnel ripped into the last redneck and he hit the deck with a heavy thrump.

Judy jumped over the bar and pressed the pistol to the bartender's head.

"What do you want?" cried the bartender, his voice quavering.

"Pow!" Judy shouted, and cocked the gun back as though having squeezed off a shot. But she hadn't.

Kev began laughing, and the mad laughter was contagious, for Judy started in with her own hilarity. The bartender chuckled nervously. Judy lifted the pistol from his head, but then brought it down hard and he stumbled and the laughter rose and Judy hit him with the pistol a second time. Again and again the pistol plummeted into his head, and the blows kept coming until the bartender dropped to the floor.

He lay behind the bar, and Judy aimed the gun and fired. His face exploded in blood.

Kev and Judy, hand and hand, ran out the door and into the lot and hopped, literally, into their convertible and Kev slammed his foot on the gas and the bright-red sports car turned and squealed, spitting out dirt in the rear, and gunned it forward, flying out of the lot.

Poetry

I don't understand people. Don't understand how to interact with them. Why do I even bother trying? Their ways are so foreign to me. Like I'm an alien, from another planet. Like I have fins growing out of my back and long feelers sticking up from my head and webbed feet that slap against the ground as I walk. They look at me like I'm some kind of freak, when all I really want is to be human like everybody else.

The Bullet

I hear the cock of a shotgun,

the click of a rifle,

the crack of a handgun;

the sound the hammer makes when it snaps the platform.

The gun fires a shot,

the powder explodes,

the sound hard and sharp,

the bullet blows out the muzzle and searches for a mark.

The target ruptures upon impact,

the bullet cuts right through,

and I see it coming and start running for my life.

The bullet is fast,

and I don't think I can evade it,

159

Jeremy Void

but I can try,

and so I try,

and my heart hammers inside.

Deadly to Be Trendy

Follow the cool kids.

Go to where the action is nonexistent:

the street corner,

the abandoned warehouse,

the deserted avenue,

the ghost town,

around the corner from Hell—

the place where God only comes

in a plastic bag.

Wrapped in tinfoil.

Sell your soul to the Devil

and spit in the eyes of your maker.

Sell yourself.

Jeremy Void

Pray that God doesn't allow you

in the Land of the Lord.

No cool kids there.

Dive headfirst into the fiery abyss.

Impulses! Don't think.

Act.

Action without thought means fun, fun, fun.

The TV tells us to be dumb.

Dude, don't do that;

do this.

Pop pills.

Stick a spike into your arm

and push down on the plunger and watch

through red eyes your life wash away in hot water.

Make waves, break rules,

break bones, and throw your life down the tube.

Take a dive.

Disintegrate.

It's what the cool kids do.

Follow the trend.

Say no to life and yes to death.

Ride the Grim Reaper.

Welcome him into your life and

Deadly to Be Trendy

say goodbye to your friends.

It's the fabulous way of the cool kids.

Decipher That, You Fuck!

The clock face ticks,

and tocks,

and I wish it would stop.

Boredom creeps up on me like a desperate whore,

a woman willing to do anything for a bag of crack cocaine.

I envy these women, for they are free.

They can do anything they want …

or need …

to do to get by.

I don't really envy them.

I mean, why would I?

They are enslaved to a plastic bag,

which spews lies about life,

Decipher That, You Fuck!

and I don't know why I ever bothered.

Like is a bore, and that I can't ignore.

I sit here with a book, reading words on a page,

but the words are meaningless to me.

They don't make sense.

My mind races like a couple competing cocks.

My brain mocks me and my futile ways,

telling me not to bother,

for I won't ever be paid.

I recognize this,

but still I write,

and I will write

until the pen dies,

and when it dies,

the sentence will be severed,

alluding to nothing and nowhere.

An endless phrase.

I am

That's where I'll stop,

because I'm sick of this story;

it's so fucking boring.

But I'm lucky to be alive.

In a way, I guess you could say.

Jeremy Void

I'm a loner in a crowd,

surrounded by millions of milling people.

I'm a king who lost his crown.

I left it at home.

And if my head weren't connected to my neck,

I'd probably lose that too.

So, the million-dollar question:

Who am I?

Who am I? Who are you?

Don't point your finger at me

or I'll break it into two.

But in the end

I know I'll always lose.

So why bother?

Decipher that, you fuck!

The Flame Dance

The flame dances as death comes nearer.

The electricity coursing through keeps it alive,

and getting dearer.

The other candle, the one representing life—

the life I have, the life that's dying—

it fades out and is forgotten about.

The death flame grows and glowers.

The life inside me ebbs as I suck in

another drag.

Another cup of coffee, another bad habit.

Another wasted day, and the death flame leers.

It dances in laughter, taunting me.

The flame of life is snuffed … out.

Fuck You

Fuck politically-correctness.

Fuck overly sensitive left-wing commies,

telling me what is and what isn't politically correct.

Fuck right-wing religious fanatics.

Most of them are too old to be believing in imaginary friends.

Fuck missionaries,

annoying preachers, preaching about how much they love Jesus.

Don't they know Jesus hates faggots.

If there is a God, fuck him too.

Fuck the government.

Fuck Obama,

just another thieving nigger destroying our country,

robbing us of our freedom.

Fuck You

Fuck all forms of politics:

social, economical, etc.

They cause more problems than they'll ever fix.

Fuck the lies told to us as kids.

Fuck the lies taught to us in school.

Fuck the land of the free because I haven't found it yet.

Our founding fathers were gun-toting drunken assholes who loved whores.

Fuck society for taking those values away.

Fuck society for taking everything away.

Fuck cops, fuck cops, fuck cops,

enforcing unjust laws.

Fuck the rest of the world for hating this country and thinking they're better.

You don't see foreigners risking their lives to live in your country.

And fuck foreigners who risk their lives to be in this country

and *still* think their country is better.

Fuck racism.

Fuck reverse-racism.

Get over it.

Fuck white liberal guilt.

I never owned a slave.

I'm a kike.

Jeremy Void

My people were slaves before there was such a word as slavery.

Fuck me,

and most of all, fuck you.

I Don't Wanna Die

When a door is slammed, a window is smashed, and I cut myself
on the jagged glass.

I emerge on the battlefield.

Where'd everybody go? I ask as I man my rifle in a gray mist amid all
the dead bodies.

The war was fought and has gone away.

With nobody left to fight I raise my rifle and press the muzzle to
my—wait, I don't wanna die.

I hold onto my sanity like a crying child, patting its back and
saying, *Everything will be okay.*

Spewing lies that dissipate before my eyes, I fall to my knees and
cry, praying that God will take away this pain, saying, *Everything will
be okay.*

I rest my head on my pillow and pray another day will make me
sane—

because the war was fought and has gone away, and I'm too late.

But another day is coming and I'm running to my bed and set my head on my pillow and pray another day will make me sane, because everything will be okay.

Jaded

I'm a pretty boy with corrupted ideals.

My face is dirty, but my thoughts are real.

What you see now is all you will see:

just a snot-nosed kid with rotting teeth.

I've dreamed of love, but dreams deceive.

All the love I'm giving you is all you'll receive.

I've got no remorse for shit I've done in the past.

If I've apologized to you, then I'm sorry 'bout that.

I'm not a poor kid and never was.

I can't fight, and I'm not too tough.

But I'll say what I want and do as I say.

If you've got a problem with that, come up to my face.

I've got dreams of ruling the whole human race.

Jeremy Void

I just wanna kill everyone who stands in my way.

Again, dreams deceive and hope is fake.

If you've got what I want, I will take.

I'm not a bad kid, but I'm not good.

I'm just a stupid kid who's been misunderstood.

Just for Kicks

I wear steel toes just for kicks.

I dress in a way that'll make you sick.

I go around acting like a total prick.

And I do it all just for kicks.

Locked In

The chains rattle

as I yank my arms away,

but their hold pulls me back

and keeps me bound to this wall.

I would try and run,

but the shackles clasped to my ankles

would make me fall and shatter

my skull on the floor.

How'd I get here?

How could I have done it again?

Again and again

I keep making the same mistakes.

I know this cell

Locked In

and the writing on the walls

better than I know myself,

and of that I'm quite ashamed.

Yet I brag about my faults,

about my downfalls and my defects,

because perfection as you know it

is a fairy tale that my mom and dad told me

when I was a wee little kid.

And I believed the stories,

thought riches and fortunes were in my future,

and yet here I am,

chained to myself

and I hate myself.

My Life

I watch my life pass me by.

It moves as quick and fluid as a snake.

It slithers and its tongue trills

as it cranes its neck to take one last look.

Its eyes are black as led, and its lips,

curving around its face as it smiles, are red

as the slash running across my wrist.

Its stare, the stare of life, cuts through me

like razor blades dipped in lemon juice.

My eyes start to leak, my eyelids droop.

The whole world is spinning and jiving.

My legs wobble and I drop down, straight down.

I let the tentacles of death embrace me.

My Life

I let them tear up my clothes, rip holes in my skin,

inject drugs into my bloodstream.

My life, your life, our life, it's gone, gone, gone.

It passed us, the two of us, by.

The Same Old Song

Clones.

Drones.

Everything's the same.

Whatever happened to going against the grain?

Do something new,

something unique.

I'm sick and tired of the same fucking track.

The same old song.

The same notes, the same chords.

It's getting old.

Gonna gimme an ulcer.

When will it stop?

I'm sick of being the only one,

The Same Old Song

the only man willing to stand out,

willing to do something new,

something unique.

This fucking tune is gonna make me puke.

I've heard it before.

I'm hearing it now.

I'll hear it again.

Shut the fuck up and break a norm.

Now, now, now!!!

You're pissing me off.

Make it stop.

Who won't you stop?

Copy cat.

You're a copy cat.

It's getting old.

It's the same old track.

Different day, different hour.

But that same song I hear every hour.

This poem sucks.

That's a fact.

But at least I have the balls to take a chance.

To stand up here and call you a cunt.

You fucking cunt.

Jeremy Void

You fucking cliché.

Clones.

Drones.

Everything's the same.

Whatever happened to going against the grain?

Does your brain not work?

Scatterbrained

My thoughts are scattered,

moving faster than my brain can catch,

a haphazard array of a million shooting thoughts,

a bouncy ball that just can't be caught.

I try and I try, but my ideas are lost.

The lines on the page jump like jagged waves.

I touch my pen to the line, but it dodges each attempt,

so I try and I try,

but the lines,

so wild and relentless, match the pace of my nervous heart,

a pounding so loud,

so haphazard   a disaster

that my pulse spikes and my head—

Jeremy Void

yikes!

A crazy rhythm—

a crazy, crass, spasmodic and fast mess that only I myself made,

my thoughts cashing checks that my brain can't catch.

An uproarious outerworld in my head,

a surreal sort of plane that I dread,

über chaos and crude thinking, I can't stop blinking,

my lips are tweaking,

my vision vile and wild, moving like a shooting star.

Because of this, you see—

although I don't—

my art looks like vomit,

so detestable like smeared feces,

though in a way it looks great, so remarkably fake.

It represents a side of me that I hate.

It's almost like standing onstage and farting into the mike,

then deemed a genius by fools alike.

I guess it would be cruel to say

stupidity is a sickness that sticks at birth,

a variety of understated answers—none the wiser—

and I look for my answers by getting higher.

I guess it would be sick to say

my brain is cement;

Scatterbrained

my brain is lazy, fat, yet so intelligent.

A question about this, and a question about that,

a harsh sound sounding so hard in my head;

so sharp and fierce,

I feel on fire,

too many burning desires,

too many futile reasons,

such pointless force—

a hellion of ideas.

Sometimes, I must admit—though I'm sorry about this—

I feel completely compelled to spray you with the truth.

But take my word for it that

the truth coming from me is neurotically sane,

though everything I do, it's all unimaginably vain.

The human race is corrupt,

it's in our nature,

it's a disaster of attachments,

a fragmented theory,

existential proof that at once proves there's a point to all this.

Something Like a Beast

The room is dark and stark,

a padded cell where hopelessness breeds.

A straightjacket strapped to my back,

so tight that I can't breathe.

I try to escape, but the key is gone,

and it's something like a beast that won't go away,

no matter how hard I try.

Every attempt is stark,

and sparks a vicious war,

a hole in my head,

a wound full of dread,

a bed for my excessive ways,

a place where I can wage **war,**

Something Like a Beast

where I can wage **hell,**

where I can chime the bells to inform you

that hell is here,

it's hell on earth,

chaos the human race deserves.

Desert me.

Leave me bleeding and dead;

like road-kill, my stomach's crushed and ill.

Do I deserve this?

The answer is clear.

Hell is here.

It's hell on earth.

The rifles play the anthem of the day,

the chaos we breed,

the chaos we need,

the chaos we see,

the chaos in our minds.

We need a place to go, where we can destroy....

We need an answer to the madness that shines from our eyes,

glowing red and grim,

thin with rage,

thick with hate,

sick with repulsion.

Jeremy Void

Destruction.

Destruction.

Death and destruction.

We need a place to defy you,

where we can wage **war,**

where we can wage **hell,**

where we can chime the bells to inform you

that hell is here,

it's hell on earth,

chaos the human race neeeeeeeeds …

if we want to live free.

To the Girl I Love

My penis sticks up and points to the one I love.

Her crisp nipples jut out and lock onto my swollen heart.

The water runs and splashes inside the tub.

She stands beneath the spray, looking like a shimmering angel,

while I stay dry and keep my eyes aligned with hers.

An angel, so sweet and naked, her skin so dark and bare,

her hair so long and wet and stuck to her shoulders like a coat of
fur.

This is the girl I love, standing nude in the tub,

her skin wet, oh so wet, and ready for me to touch.

I step forward and plant my hands on her shoulders.

My erect penis applies pressure to her slightly rounded belly.

Her body deflects the spray of water coming down hard on her
head,

and I take it in the face and start to shiver, my bones trembling and
cold.

This must be the reason why her nipples are hard.

I took it as a sign that she loves me as much as I love her.

I step closer and wrap my arms around her back.

My penis shrinks a bit as her body pushes it straight facing up.

I feel it squeezed tightly between us as we hug.

I look down, and I'm on the verge of crying out loud.

I look down at the voluptuous rump jutting out from behind her.

I feel her pubic hair brushing against my skin,

rubbing against my leg like a wet and soggy sponge.

The feeling so sweet and sensual that

I cry and I cry, knowing not the reason why.

Maybe because the spray of cold water,

raining down with the force of a fly swatter,

juxtaposed against the warmth of her body—

her firm tits, her soft skin,

her wiry arms gripping me tight,

her head flush with my chest,

her cheek pressed to my peck—

it's so unreal, so surreal, like it's too good to be true.

Why me? is what I'm thinking as tears stream down my face.

The soap in my hair dissipates with the heavy flow of water.

To the Girl I Love

My penis shrinks and hardens, standing straight up between us.

Her warm body. Her hard nipples—

I feel them poking holes in my skin, cutting crevices in my chest,

carving a path to my heart, so that she can see what's inside.

Dooooon't!!! You won't like what you'll find.

She tells me not to worry, but cringes when she catches

my cold heart in her line of sight.

It's blue, she says, so very blue, and frozen solid, not even beating.

Your heart is cold, she tells me, like I didn't already know,

as her nipples harden and sharpen and look like the barrels of two
loaded guns.

Jeremy Void

My Punk Rock Rutland

A **friend of mine asked** to interview me on the Rutland Punk scene, for a paper he had to write for school. Here is the result of said interview, in its original form:

How/when did you discover Punk in Rutland?

A little over three years ago, when I was fairly new to Rutland, Vermont, I went to the FYE at the mall here. As I was standing in line waiting to buy a belt buckle, the young, freckly-faced guy working the register said, You're a real Punk.

Though I don't recall my exact response, I said something along the lines of Who, me?

You're not from Rutland, are you?

No, I'm from Boston.

We got talking and he revealed his affiliations with the Midnight Saints—for he, it turned out, was their guitarist, Mike—and I might have mentioned I formerly sang for Lethal Erection. One

193

thing led to another and he asked me if I would sing for the Midnight Saints, which in the end never happened.

What changes have you seen since?
At my first Punk show in Rutland, I started a raucous mosh pit, and the crowd went crazy, spiraling out of control to the rapid drumbeat, the fast guitar riff, the window-shattering bass, and the crass vocals of some ugly cunt. There it was, a human tornado, in which I drove my bony elbow into some dude's eye—hey, he shouldn't have gotten in my way—and severed another dude's glasses. I had fun, to say the least. But as time progressed and I decided to give sobriety a shot, the mosh pits at the UU started to dissipate. There was a period of time when I couldn't mosh because this crowd of young girls hogged the floor and I didn't want to knock them over.

When I went to see the Misfits play in upstate New York, I had a sudden, startling realization that I was no longer a kid. After hitting on a few teenage girls and getting shot down each time, wondering what was wrong, it came to me while I was dancing in the pit: I was an adult and I was the oldest one dancing and they all probably thought I was a creep. Which I am, but they didn't need to know.

I'm not saying I'm the reason the mosh pits in Rutland lack life these days; I'm just saying that with my absence from the dance floor they aren't what they once were. That, or they're back to what they once were. Either way, without my involvement the world is an awful place. Look what happened to Reagan.

More changes have occurred than just the death of the slam dance in Rutland. Like the Midnight Saints losing and gaining members; the arrival of new bands; Cozy Cum's changing their sound. The show Dianne cancelled because This Time Stars Fall booked the same night at the Knights of Columbus. And more.

What connections have you made outside Rutland via the scene in Rutland?

To be honest, as far as the scene's concerned, both in Boston and in Rutland, I'm dead. I left Boston and a year later went to see the Business at Club Lido in Boston, where I saw a lot of my old friends. That night I got so wasted and felt like a fucking king. I showed up with a little over $100 and spent all my money on beer. Joe gave me half a pint of whiskey. Not to mention all the liquor I drank for free. People kept coming up to me and asking me where I've been. I told them the truth, which was an outright lie. I claimed to have just gotten out of prison. Like all ex-convicts, I was a king to all the scumbags there. Free booze, free booze, and free adoration. My point is, Rutland hasn't helped me make connections; it has only hindered me.

How do you find out about shows?

Simply, I find shows by drinking as much beer as possible, shooting dope, smoking crack, and snatching a purse from a helpless old lady. All fucked up and feeling the adrenaline drawn from theft, I stumble around town until finally I accidentally stumble through the doors of the show and instantly I'm home.

How has the town of Rutland itself impacted your taste in music?

Rutland hasn't impacted my taste in music, but I'm sure I've impacted theirs, because I'm just that great.

What is the significance of a Punk scene existing in a small town?

Every town, big or small, can benefit from the energy provided by Punk. A town without Punk, I'd have to say, is boring. I don't know what I'd do if Punk never found me and stole me away on its magic carpet of rebellion. I'd have killed myself by now. I hate life enough *with* the existence of Punk. Without it would be like a bullet to my ball sack. Imagine standing on a chair with one of its legs broken and there's a noose around your neck. If the chair tips, you're dead. You're stuck. Imagine that. Now, tell me what that's got to do with Punk.

How do you think others perceive Punk?

I don't really care how others perceive Punk. Not good, I'd assume. But each one of those assholes looking down on Punks are probably at home shooting dope and smoking crack and drinking themselves to death while we're out drinking to live, fighting for kicks, and living it up. Fuck those boring cunts! They mean as much to me as the scum beneath my shoes and the plaque on my teeth.

My Punk Rock Rutland

What do you predict for the future of the scene?

The future? Don't you know the world's going to end in only a few more years? I've known that since I was just a little kid. But, anyway, the future is like toilet paper.

What is Punk?

Lastly, Punk is my home. A lot of people find Punk; Punk found me. I'm a true misfit, a fuckup by nature; I was Punk when I was only in diapers. By that I don't mean my parents were in the scene and thought I'd look cute with a Mohawk, *Thurston*. I'm speaking metaphorically, of course. I never fit in with my peers. The first place I remember feeling a sense of belonging was at my second Punk show. I went there without a single friend in the world and went home with a million of them. The greatest thing about being Punk is it gives one a license to be a mess. The definition of the word "Punk" is someone who is mean, dirty, a kid who you don't want your daughter to date—my favorite combination of words, "crude, rude, and lewd"—but that definition is so farfetched from what a Punk rocker actually is. In the seventies Punks adopted that label because it's what outsiders were already calling them so why not make it official? I'm a lazy slob, I pick my nose, I spit when I walk, I scratch my balls in public; not to mention all the crimes I've committed and my high school reputation—my reputation on the streets, too. My knack for breaking things—unintentionally, of course—and the billion other things wrong with me. "I don't got a pretty face. I don't care what you say. I don't got a pretty face. To me you're a fucking disgrace. I don't got the greatest ideas. But I'll shove them in your face like diarrhea. I don't got the greatest ideas. To me they're fucking grand."

197

Jeremy Void

About the Author

Jeremy Void was born and raised in Boston, MA, where he played in a Punk rock band called Lethal Erection and stirred up chaos everywhere he went. Friends, enemies, and followers alike called him "St. Chaos," and he kept up his reputation at all times, finding the funny side of just about everything, and leading a life of misadventures that eventually led him down a rocky road to Rutland, VT, where he resides for the time being, writing short stories.